THE GREEN GIRL

By
JACK WILLIAMSON

I0616937

ARMCHAIR FICTION
PO Box 4369, Medford, Oregon   97501-0168

*For more information about Armchair Books and products, visit our
website at…*

www.armchairfiction.com

Or email us at…

armchairfiction@yahoo.com

THE DAY THE SUN WAS KIDNAPPED!

At high noon on May 4th the sun went out. And at that moment the youthful Melvin Dane was thrust into the most amazing adventure ever encountered by a mortal man. For years he had dreamed of a beautiful green-skinned girl, and now that dream of love was to materialize into a threat that held the promise of death for every living being on Earth. To meet the challenge of a blacked-out world, Mel followed a scientific trail that led to dangers undreamed of: a horrific serpent-like creature; a red globe of atomic destruction, murderous zombies, silver globes of sudden death, and strange dragon plants. All of this awaits you in Jack Williamson's powerful novel, "The Green Girl," a true masterpiece from the golden age of science-fiction.

FOR A COMPLETE SECOND NOVEL, TURN TO PAGE 129

CAST OF CHARACTERS

MEL DANE

His boyhood dreams of a green-skinned girl had seemed so real—and they soon materialized into a reality that mixed romantic delight with a malignant force of unspeakable horror.

XENORA

Incredibly beautiful, yet her skin was a light shade of green. She was thought to have been nothing but a dream for many years, yet her real life rescue by Mel put both of them in grave danger.

SAM WALDEN

He was a brilliant scientist—and he was Earth's only protection against an assault by an unknown, evil intelligence. His genius soon uncovered a secret inner world deep inside the ocean.

THE LORD OF THE FLAME

It lived on eternally, deep within the pit of Xath—a loathsome demon with the body of a fiery serpent, whose plans promised frozen death for all mankind!

ALEXANDER

A truly frightening creature—green wings and a head like a flower! It made a pact with Sam that led to the ultimate battle between good and evil.

CHAPTER ONE
May 4th, 1999

AT HIGH NOON on May 4, 1999, the sun went out! It had risen bright and clear. The summer sky had had an unwonted liquid brilliance. The climbing daystar had shone all the morning with unusual intensity. But just at ten o'clock, an intangible mist obscured the sky! A pale and deepening film stole over the crystal infinity of the heavens. The sky assumed a dull, almost copper tinge, which developed into a ghastly scarlet pall! In five minutes the sky changed from a soft and limpid blue to an intense, darkling scarlet. In the appalling suggestion of blood in the dusky crimson depths, there was a grim omen of the fate of Earth!

I had got up at dawn for a plunge in the surf, and all the morning I had been wandering about the bit of beach and the strip of virgin woodland behind it, content in the restful, soothing peace of that untouched bit of Nature, rejoicing lazily in the vivid greenness of it, in the fresh odors of earth and plant, in the whisper of the wind in the palms. I lounged on the crisp grass in the cooling shade, living in my sympathy with the life about me, watching the long soft rollers of the green-blue Atlantic surging deliberately toward the crystal whiteness of the sunlit sandy beach. The soft cerulian skies were clear, save for the white wings of occasional airships that glanced in the bright sunshine. The morning had a singularly quiet and soothing beauty. My sleepy soul was in harmony with the distant mellow chime of a church bell. I lay back in the peaceful rest of a man ready to sink lazily into the evening of life.

Though I am still an able man of somewhat less than thirty years, I felt that morning none of the energetic exuberance or youth. I felt something of the age and the agelessness of Nature herself. I felt no fires of ambition; I was oddly devoid of feeling or emotion; I felt content to steep my soul for eternities in Nature's simple wonders. But I have always been a dreamer.

I was a worshiper come unknowingly for the last time to the shrine of life. For even then the doom was gathering! But I was spared all knowledge of the alien menace that was blotting out the sun. I had no premonition that within a few short hours the balmy Florida coast would be a frozen wilderness, whipped with bitter winds and lashed with freezing seas!

I had risen at last, and was sauntering down the hard white sand in the direction of our cottage, listening idly to the birds—singing on the eve of their doom. I came in sight of the house, a low building, covered with climbing vines and half-hidden in the trees. I strolled toward it upon the narrow, curving gravel walk, lost in the peace of the rustic setting.

The Doctor was sitting on the small veranda, gazing sleepily out over the sea, with his pipe in his mouth and his hands on the arms of his chair. Dr. Samuel Walden was the sole person in the world, outside the vivid creations of my dreams, for whom I had affection. He was an unusual character. Born in 1929, he was now seventy years of age. His earlier life had been devoted to science, and he had won fame and fortune for himself by the invention of the hydrodyne sub-atomic engine. But in the last twenty years he had done no scientific work—or so I thought, for I had never been behind the little door that he kept always locked.

A close friend of my parents, he had been more than a father to me since they were lost in the turmoil of the last outbreak against the Council of Nations, when I was three years old. We had always lived in the old cottage on the hill, in this natural park on the Florida coast. He loved Nature deeply. For many years his chief interests in life had been plants and animals, for which he cared more than for society. A flower, a dog, the sound of the surf—such things were the joys of his life.

Though his hair had been white for many years, his lean, tanned face was unwrinkled, and he was among the strongest men of my acquaintance. In fact, two years before, he had won second place at the Olympic wrestling contests. He loved the simple things of life. He had a passion for cooking, and he made it a science as well as an art. He was an inveterate smoker, and clung to the habit, even when he had to have the tobacco smuggled in from Asia at vast expense. He had an old music box, of a type that went out of date half a century ago, to which he used to listen for hours on end.

There was little enough about Sam Walden's daily life to show that he was the greatest scientist of the Earth, and the sole hope for the world in the amazing battle that was brewing. His simple philosophy had changed him far from the energetic young inventor of the hydrodyne. No one would have suspected the qualities of supreme heroism that he revealed.

During the days of my youth we had restlessly wandered over the globe. We had lived rather aimlessly—for the simple joy of living. The mountains, the desert, and the sea have always had a fascinating call for both of us, and we wandered in answer to that call—and during some of those years, I traveled on a strange quest of my own.

But it was a whole decade since we had left our rustic home.

And as our latter years had been quiet and tranquil, so the world had lost the fierce energy and struggle for advancement that had driven it during Sam's younger days. It had settled down to the enjoyment of peaceful content. Science had turned from the invention of new machines to the improvement of those in existence, and had died with their perfection, until, when the crisis came, Sam was the only man on Earth able to understand and to cope with it!

The industrial organization had been perfected. Work was done by machines. Men attended them for short hours and played through long ones. There were no rich, and no poor. The products of industry were fairly divided. All men received their shares in content and enjoyed them to the full, without troubling themselves about the questions of science or religion or of lift that had received the attention of the past generation.

And upon the peaceful tranquility of that happy, prosperous age, there fell with no warning the lurid doom that no man could explain, throwing it into frenzied confusion. In the past era, there would have been a thousand men to attack the problem, with all the power of clear, dynamic minds. Now, there was just *one man* who could understand!

It was not so much that scientific knowledge was lacking.

Men still studied and talked the language of science. The machines demanded it. But there were none of the trained and penetrating minds, used to departing boldly from the world of the known to bring forth the new. Science was no longer living. It was mechanical.

CHAPTER TWO
The Radio Girl

I HAVE SAID that I am a dreamer, living more truly in my fancy than in the world. Perhaps my imagination is abnormally developed. Always I have had new worlds awaiting me in my dreams, to which I could retire when life was dull or unattractive. My visions have always had a singular reality, such a definite concreteness, that it sometimes seemed to be the truth.

The old wonder stories of Wells and Verne, and of the pseudo-scientific writers of the first part of this century have always appealed to me. I had a vast collection of ancient volumes and tattered magazines, full of those old stories, which I read and reread with passionate interest. The rest of the world had forgotten them with the passing of the age of science, but I found in them the priceless food of fancy.

Psychologists say that many children have dream companions of some kind. They are very real entities of the child's imagination, playmates of fancy. They usually fade and are forgotten as the adolescent child becomes absorbed in the activities of life, and the imagination atrophies.

Since the days of my earliest recollections, I have visited in the world of my dreams a wonderful playmate. It is a girl, with dark brown hair, deep, warm violet eyes, and clear skin, so I thought, slightly tinged with green, though the lips were very red. I have always thought that she was very beautiful, and she has always been very real to me.

And the vision did not fade as the years went by! Still I visited the Green Girl, as I called her, in my fancy, and she replaced many of the normal childhood interests that I might have had. It is because of her that I have always been happiest when I was silent and alone; it is because of my dreams that I have been inclined to avoid the society of others.

The strange world of dreams in which I visited her was very real to me, a place of weird wonders, sometimes of alien terrors, in which the Green Girl and I wandered through interminable, astounding adventures. And I have always had an unaccountable persuasion that it was a real world, somewhere, through which my mind roamed in such delightful fancies!

It was twenty years ago, when I was just five years old, that the Green Girl first came into my dreams. Sam had rigged up, for my edification, an old-fashioned radio set, with headphones. In the long, lonely silences of the warm Florida nights, when a less indulgent guardian would have had me in bed, I sat up with those old phones on my ears, exploring the ether, feeling near the infinite mystery of space. I listened with childish intentness to the odd noises of the static, eagerly dreaming of calls from other planets.

It was during one of those long still nights that I first entered that world of fancy, and found—the Green Girl. It seemed that I heard first a cry of delight in a silver voice, and then she was with me. She was but a tiny sprite, smaller than myself. She seemed to stand before me, smiling at me, tossing her dark curls, with the light of bright intelligence in her blue-violet eyes. I loved her from the first. She was very beautiful. Her skin had just a tinge of green, like a tinted photograph; it did not seem a strange color. The vision was very real to me.

When she spoke—and I half imagined her words were really coming over the ether—there was a childish lisp in her voice, but still a ring of confidence and courage. Her words were strange, but I soon grew to sense their meaning, almost by intuition. Night after night, when I put on the phones and tuned in on the strange noises of the ether, that vision came back. It was not long before I could speak that strange tongue as fluently as I could speak English.

With childish reserve, I told Sam nothing about my wonderful dream, until one day he heard me chattering in the language I had learned. He questioned me eagerly; and I shyly told him all about it, and even supplied material for a grammar of the language. He took a keen scientific interest in the matter, when he learned that the vision came only over the radio, and he began to formulate theories of telepathic suggestion and mind control by ether waves.

The matter was written up by a prominent psychologist to whom he reported it. The account appeared in a well-known scientific magazine, with comments upon the strange language, which, oddly enough, bore not the slightest similarity to any known tongue, and appeared rather too perfect to be credited to the invention of a five-year-old. The writer mentioned Sam's ideas, that I had established telepathic contact with another planet, or perhaps with the far-distant past or future; but theories of mind reading received little welcome in a day when science was dormant, and even the suggestion that the language, became of its simplicity, power, and labial beauty, would become the long-sought international tongue, was soon completely forgotten.

But I did not forget the Green Girl. The conviction grew upon me that she was a real living entity. To find her became my ruling passion. Under Sam's tutelage I poured over geographical accounts, searching in vain for some clue to a hidden nation. But the fact that the language seemed to have no sister tongue on Earth discouraged that. Between my tenth and fifteenth years Sam and I restlessly scoured the globe in search of a clue but, a decade before, we had given it up.

I turned to dreams of interplanetary travel, with a passionate desire to explore space and venture to other worlds in search of my dream girl; but the space flier seemed as far in the future as it had been a hundred years before. To please me, however, Sam helped design and construct a model of a machine we called the Omnimobile—because it should be able to travel in all elements.

But, as the years of my early manhood passed, I slowly relinquished all hope of finding the Green Girl in fact, and resolved to content myself with her companionship in fancy. It was then, too, that I developed my inordinate fondness for scientific romances, which I devoured insatiably to feed my dreams. It was only during the first few years that I could find her only over the radio. As time went by, she became an inseparable companion of my mind.

Once, for a time, I tried to lose myself in science. I had Sam teach me chemistry, but that could not replace my dreams.

Together, the Green Girl and I went through ten thousand fantastic adventures. It was as if our two minds met in the world of dreams jointly created by both of us. Certainly it was influenced by the incidents of my life, and by the wonder tales I read. And the girl told me stories, strange and thrilling narratives they were, of mythical heroes of her race that struggled with weird terrors.

She grew up with myself, until she became a princess of incomparable beauty. Often I have wished that I were a gifted painter, that I might have tried to record her charms, but even if I had been such, her perfection would have discouraged my efforts. She was slender, erect, combining an unconscious dignity of poise with vivacious sprightliness of manner. Her hair was soft and curly and brown. Her pale green skin was very soft; her full lips very red. And her sparkling violet eyes were clear and honest—bright wells of human sympathy.

Could I believe that such a supernal being was merely a dream?

CHAPTER THREE
The Scarlet Pall

THE COMING of the terror was slow and gradual enough—and as silent as the tomb! With all the magic of the quiet woodland beauty throbbing in my being, I was strolling up the narrow gravel walk toward the peaceful vine-covered cottage, where Sam was sitting in sleepy content. Gazing idly into the measureless infinity of the liquid azure sky, I saw the beginning come, so slowly that I scarcely marked it.

A pale rosy mist seemed suddenly to condense in the sky! A ubiquitous crimson haze was born from nowhere. Even as I stood in open-mouthed amazement—with the sudden chill of alien terror grasping my limbs and tugging at my heart— the hue of the sky ran quickly from the pure deep blue to an intense and awful scarlet! It was deeper than the crimson of sunset—it had a terrible, bloody intensity. It was as if a spray of blood from the arteries of some dying monster had abruptly encrimsoned the sky.

A fearful, blood-red twilight fell swiftly upon the tranquil beauty of the scene before me, painting it with hues of weird and gruesome horror. The once blue sea rolled in like a tide of blood, flashing a million gleams of awful crimson light, as the red sun was reflected on its waves. Familiar objects took on dreadful forms of wild foreboding, in that suddenly ghastly gloom of red!

And that was but the beginning.

The Unknown is always terrible, and if ever the Earth was menaced with an unfamiliar threat, it was that scarlet pall. For a moment I was gripped fast by the surprise, and the chilling, alien fear of it. Then my reason reasserted itself, and I hurried on toward the cottage, trying to convince myself that my dread was unfounded.

I knew, of course, that red light penetrated clouds much better than other colors. I knew that the red light of a neon beacon is visible through miles of mist. I knew that the sun looks red on a murky day, because all but the red rays are absorbed by the atmosphere. I had an idea that a cloud had suddenly come between Earth and sun, perhaps a haze of meteoric dust. But I failed to reassure myself.

With a glance at the sun, which was gleaming at the zenith like a great red moon, I stepped upon the veranda, still feeling a slight weakness about the knees. Sam had risen to his feet. He stood gazing silently and blankly out to the eastern horizon, where the flaming intensity of the encrimsoned sky met the glancing brilliant beams from the darkened sea. There was no surprise in his expression, and little of fear—merely pain and despair.

"What is it, Sam?" I asked quickly.

He looked around slowly. "I don't know what it is, Mel, but it means the end of the Earth! I've known for years that it was coming, but I hoped it wouldn't be so soon."

"You knew that this was coming? And you didn't tell anybody? Not even me?"

"It would have done no good. What would be the benefit to mankind to know that it was doomed to die like rats in a trap? A few more years and I might have been ready to save the Earth. As it is, there's just a chance—a bare chance!"

"But what does it mean? It's uncanny!"

He sat down again, wearily. There were lines of age and care on his lean face that I had never seen before. But even in the dull red light, there was still energy and determination in it.

"I've never told you, Mel, but ever since the radio brought you your dream of the Green Girl, I have been working—building delicate apparatus and exploring the ether. And I found a strange force at work—a force that is battling to control the ether. For fifteen years I have known that it was working *to freeze the Earth.*"

"To freeze the Earth?"

"It seems so. What it is, is a mystery whose solution has resisted all my efforts. I can hardly conceive a reason for it. But I know that something is at work to cut us off from the sun. You know that light waves of different phases and the same frequency interfere, with mutual extinction—the diffraction grating is based on that fact. And interfering waves have been setting up such a disturbance in the ether about the Earth as will ultimately cut off the sun's radiation! The principles of it are a bit abstruse. Even now, of course, the effect is only partially complete. In fact, the red and infra-red rays carry most of the sun's heat."

"Then there's no immediate danger?"

"No man knows at what moment the force may be synchronized. When it is, within a short time the temperature of the Earth will fall to absolute zero. And even as it is, life could not go on long under this red pall, for all life depends upon the actinic rays in the ultra-violet spectrum."

"And you have kept a thing like this to yourself for years?"

"It would have done the world no good to know that any day might be its last. I have spared no efforts to find means of averting the catastrophe. And it has been terrible to know. Every day that I have walked among our trees, or listened to the birds, or watched the wonder of the sea, I have known that in a day it might all be frozen death!"

"But you say there is a chance? There's something you can do to save the Earth?"

"I've built a machine to broadcast vibrations to interfere with that other force. It will upset it—I hope—for perhaps a few days. But think, Mel, what it means. Think of the vastness the power that would be able to cut off the sun! Earth—mankind—would mean nothing to it. It would soon get around my interference. I must save my machine for the last emergency."

CHAPTER FOUR
The Amazing Night

THE ONLY difference between red and blue light is that the waves of the red are about twice as long as the others. There must have been a sort of screen in the ether that somehow intercepted all but a narrow band of frequencies in the red, the other wavelengths being either canceled or converted into vibrations too long or too short to be perceptible. If there was such a screen, it was slowly altered, so that the lengths of the penetrating waves became shorter and shorter.

In other words, the color of the sky slowly ran through all the colors of the spectrum toward the blue! The sun changed from a vast round blood-ruby to a blazing yellow diamond, flooding the Earth with a sodium light! To an emerald, huge and supernally bright, coloring the sea and the sky with a dim and ghastly green radiance! The green melted into a cold and awful blue! The frozen sapphire slowly turned violet! And the violet sun grew soft and dim—and dim—until it went out utterly!

The heavens were black at midday.

The sky was an empty, illimitable chasm of darkness. The night was almost tangible—it seemed to have an oppressive weight. It was blacker than any photographer's darkroom. Trees, cottage, sounding sea, had vanished. It made no difference to close my eyes, or to put my hand before them. A great dizziness came over me, and I groped blindly for the post of the veranda, and clung to it helplessly when I found it.

The sounds that came to me were oddly reassuring. The rustle of the wind in the palms, and the plaintive chirp of a few birds in the unseen trees, and the dull, ceaseless rumble of the waves. Then I heard a heavy sigh from Sam, and the scraping of his shoe on the floor. Then a match scratched, and a pitiful little yellow flame lit the veranda, showing Sam's lean, earnest face very clearly against the wall of night.

"Thank God we can see it burn," he muttered. "If they had exhausted the ether here, the jig would have been up with my electrical machinery."

"They? Lord! Do you think somebody—"

He looked toward me, holding up the blazing splinter. "There is the possibility—even a probability—that we have to deal with a force directed by intelligence."

"Who do you think—"

"I didn't say human intelligence."

"You mean Mars or—"

He grinned in the feeble light. "No. Nothing out of your stories. The human imagination is limited by human experience. And there are plenty of things possible that human beings have never experienced."

"What do you mean, Sam?" I gasped in utter bewilderment.

"I don't know what it is that is attacking the Earth. Possibly it is something so strange, so alien to my purely human experience that it would wreck my mind to know!" Abruptly he turned toward the door. "I must go in and get to work on the machine."

The match had burned out, and the utter blackness had fallen again. I heard the old scientist get briskly to his feet and walk into the house. He reached the light button, and the hall was flooded with cold white radiance. The bright, slender beam, thrown out across the veranda comforted me immensely; but I still stood against the post, trying vainly to think out what Sam had said.

The breeze grew cooler. In ten minutes a thin cold wind sprang up from the north. I drew my light garments close about my body and shivered a little. For a while I did not go in. Presently I felt a cold mist on the wind. Suddenly a snowflake splashed chillingly against my face—an omen of the frigid doom that lay before the Earth! I got up and stepped inside the door, to escape the icy wind. In a few minutes it began to rain, because, of course, of the chilling of the air and condensation of the moisture.

Suddenly curious about how the world was taking the weird catastrophe, and about what was happening elsewhere, I went to the radiophone in the living room, and switched it on. Not a sound came from it! Not even a hint of static. The ether was utterly dead. That meant that the strange force had already cut our civilization up into a thousand helplessly isolated units!

Then from the rear of the building I heard the peculiar rhythmic throbbing beat of a hydrodyne power generator. Sam was already at work in the little room he had always kept locked, even against me. I walked back to the door and knocked, asking to be allowed to come in.

Sam called out for me to enter, and I stepped inside. I stopped at the door in amazement. The little space was crowded with intricate electrical apparatus of modern design—in fact, much of it was new and unfamiliar to me. There were intra-atomic power generators, huge electron tubes, coils, switches, loop antenna, and a wealth of other material that was strange to me. I saw at once that the laboratory before me must have represented vast sums of money and years of toil.

Sam, clad in a pair of greasy overalls, with a great smudge of grease already over half his lean face, was working intently over a huge, complex device in the center of the room. Evidently it had been recently and hastily assembled from the materials at hand, and was not yet quite finished. In fact, a desk by the wall was still littered with the plans and calculations from which it had been set up.

It was evidently founded on an adaptation of Sam's great invention of forty years before, the hydrodyne sub-atomic engine. The hydrodyne is based in principle on the catalytic disruption, by means of a radioactive salt, of water, the products being hydrogen and oxygen gases, which are burned in the cylinders, the steam formed being condensed and pumped back into the coils. The actual energy comes from the disintegration of hydrogen atoms, and the efficiency of the device is shown by the fact that the great generators on the transoceanic aerial liners require only a half pint of water as fuel per trip.

At one end of Sam's new machine was the hydrodyne unit. From the size of the catalyzer coil, it must have been of vast capacity. The conduits led to the transformer coils, and above the coils were the giant electron tubes, six feet high, of a novel, horseshoe shape. Sam was working with deft fingers at the connections.

"It will be hours, yet," he said absently, without looking up.

For a long time I stood looking at him, as he worked with utter absorption and feverish haste. There was nothing I could do to help him—I could hardly understand what he was about. How strange it was to stand there in a freezing world and watch one lone man struggling to save it!

The cold rain was drumming heavily on the roof, and the roar of the sea had risen. The wind was blowing a gale, but there was no lightning in the storm that night. The out-of-doors was as dark as Erebus. Presently it grew cold in the room. I went out and shut the doors, and turned on the resistance heaters. Then I made a cup of coffee and brought it to Sam. He gulped it down absently, and went on without a word. I went back to my chair by the wall, and I think I must have fallen asleep.

CHAPTER FIVE
The Etheric Storm

THE NEXT THING I knew, Sam was shaking my shoulder. I sat up, rubbing my eyes, a bit dazed at first, and uncertain whether I could credit what I remembered to be a vivid nightmare. But when I looked at the utter fatigue and the intense anxiety on the old scientist's face, I knew that it was not a dream.

"I've got it adjusted now," he said. "Suppose you go outside and watch. We need to know exactly what happens. And it may fail."

As I got up awkwardly, stretching my tired limbs, he climbed on his stool before the complex array of instruments on the wall, and began to manipulate the switches and dials.

"I have just to pick up their vibrations and synchronize mine with them," he said in a voice dull with fatigue. "In five minutes we will know. With these instruments I can pick up and analyze any disturbance in the ether, whether it be Hertzian or wireless wave two miles long, or any of the shorter waves that extend down to heat or infra-red, through the visible and ultraviolet spectrums, and even below, to the Cosmic Rays. I can pick up vibrations that other scientists have merely reasoned ought to exist! I will analyze the force that is being used and then put my vibrations against it. I hope to set up an effective interference, temporarily, at least."

In two minutes I was standing out of doors, with a rug about my shoulders, in a blackness that was almost palpable. The bitter wind still blew a little, but the rain had stopped. The ground was frozen, and a light fall of snow crunched underfoot. Drawing the rug close about me, I groped my shivering way to the front of the yard, thinking of the misery and death that the cold must already have brought to Earth, realizing, for the first time, how dependent human welfare is on the whims of nature.

For a few minutes I waited in the frozen darkness, and nothing happened. Then began a fantastic thing, a veritable storm in the ether!

A faint living light of violet—blessed dawn of reborn day—came in the south; thin misty streamers of violet flame flashed through the unutterable midnight of the heavens. Violet fire flickered and burned in a pale and nebulous aurora that ran with lightning speed to the four corners of the heavens. It danced, it wavered, and it marched in gleaming pointed lances of pulsing flame!

And then the violet became a ubiquitous lucent background for a weirdly glorious and terrible play of bright, coruscating tongues of polychromatic fire. Suddenly a great blade of vivid, flaming green cut through the glowing violet, flashed across the sky in amazing splendor, and burst into a hundred blazing globes of brilliant emerald, that rolled down misty tracks of flame to the horizon.

A flickering, many-tongued sheet of amber was born in the east, spread over the violet haze throughout the heavens, and died into a pale saffron sheet that slowly changed and warmed to a rich glow of rosy mist. And from it grew a flickering wall of serpent tongues of orange, and scarlet, and blue, that danced and spread, and wove themselves into a curious crown of throbbing flame at the zenith.

All that wild and astounding storm of flame was as still as the grave. The chill wind had died. The air was keen and quiet. The snow-covered earth lay vast about me, queerly lit by the changing colors in the sky. Even the sea was silent, but living in the wonder of reflected light. All the world was quiet—as if the sun had been utterly gone, and it had been frozen indeed!

Brighter scarlet and green and purple lights burst up about the horizon in great fountains of wonderful fire, and poured through the sky in cyclonic whirls of burning splendor. It was like some vast pyrotechnic display; but the fire filled the heavens, and shone with incredibly splendid, living radiance, of every color in the spectrum—the pure and dripping essence of molten light!

Thin, feathery tongues of soft prismatic colors, great bars of intense and vivid fire, huge and rippling sheets of blinding brilliance, vast globes and vague shapes of bright and mist-edged flame, all interwoven in a Titanic storm of throbbing, flashing, iridescent light—a whirlwind of coruscating flame, splendid as a cascade of rubies and diamonds sweeping down in a sunlit stream of molten gold. A pulsing mist of woven flaming rainbows.

And suddenly there came a spot of pure, supernal blue at the zenith. Wonderful sight! It spread in a growing circle of blessed light. In a moment the last faint tinge of crimson fire was fading on the northern horizon. The skies were blue again!

The sun was far past the meridian. It had been hidden thirty hours! Its clear warm rays poured over the snow-clad landscape, sparkling in white brilliance on the frost and dancing on the silent sea. It was wonderful to see the world again in daylight, to feel the genial warmth of the restored sun.

Sam had won! He had torn down the curtains in the ether, and lit the sun again!

I went back in the house and found him slumped down in a chair fast asleep, with the vestiges of a happy smile left on his face. I had not realized the strain he had been under. He had been driving himself for thirty hours like a high-speed machine. The intensity of the effort had exhausted him utterly. He did not wake up while I was putting him to bed.

In an hour the radio had come to life. The ether was buzzing like an angry beehive with reports of the catastrophe, and with mad speculations as to its cause. The red gloom, followed by the absolute darkness, had fallen simultaneously upon the entire Earth. All lines of power and communication had been put out of order, as in a severe magnetic storm, and utter panic had gripped the world. Every man had fancied himself to be among the few survivors of an unthinkable catastrophe.

A blanket of cold had fallen upon all the Earth. In many sections there had been torrential rains as the clouds condensed, and there was considerable loss of life due to flood. In certain sections there had been terrible blizzards, and thousands had been frozen to death. Vast damage had been done to young crops, and there was a threat of famine. But, in most places, enough radiation to cause freezing weather had been prevented by the dense clouds.

Varied and fantastic theories were advanced as to the cause of the unique phenomenon. The most popular explanation was that the solar system had passed through a small, dense nebula, the particles and condensing gases of which had intercepted solar radiation.

Sam's brief statement, advanced a few days later, that he had found the disturbance to be due to a strange force acting to erect etheric screen or shell about the Earth, through which vibration could not pass, received scant attention despite his scientific reputation; and his warning that it might return again at any time, and forever, passed unheeded. He made no mention of what he had done to save the Earth.

CHAPTER SIX
The Omnimobile

I NOW COME to the Omnimobile, the machine that Sam had designed with a view to use in interplanetary navigation. He had worked on it, of course, more to please me than for any other reason; and we both knew that there was little chance of the machine's being able to make a successful voyage through space.

On the day after the sun had been restored, Sam was back in his laboratory, still feeling out the strange forces in the ether, and trying to anticipate the next attack. I was wandering along the beach, rejoicing in the bright warmth of the sun, absorbing the spell of the wood and the sea and the fresh salty air, regretting that all of it might be frozen again. There an idea came abruptly to me.

Why not build the Omnimobile?

Designed to withstand the bitter cold and the absolute vacuum of space, planned to survive the shock of landing on frozen worlds, equipped to traverse the terrible mountains of the moon, to crawl over the burned deserts of Mars, or to explore the vast seas of Venus—even if it would not be able to actually leave the Earth, might it not preserve our lives when the frozen night came again?

A bitter existence it might seem, to spend one's years shut up in a metal cylinder, in a dark and frozen world, traveling, perhaps, in absolute night, over still, unseen cities of the dead. But I had my books—and the Green Girl! I could live on with that wonderful princess of my dreams, and forget the doom of my kind. It seemed selfish to think of it—but my love of the Green Girl was so great that I would have given my all for her, even to dream of her.

When I reached the cottage I spoke to Sam of my idea, and he agreed with an alacrity that surprised me. We tested the little model again, and he made revisions and alterations in the design. In a few days we began construction on the beach two hundred yards below the cottage. There was no lack of funds, and we pushed the work with all speed. We had a hundred workmen on the spot, and shops all over the country were busy turning out the parts and instruments which were rushed to us by air. I superintended the work myself, since Sam still spent most of his time in the little laboratory, working with that mysterious force.

The Omnimobile, conceived and designed by Sam, would have been worthy of a Jules Verne's creative mind, and the great adventure into which it led us was far more weirdly amazing than any of those old wonder tales to which I had so passionately devoted myself. Without the hydrodyne, and a dozen other inventions of Sam's, the machine would have been impossible. Certainly it merited the name Omnimobile, for it was hard to imagine a place to which it would not be able to go.

The vessel was of a tapering cylindrical shape, ten feet in central diameter, and forty-five feet long. The construction throughout was of the strongest modern alloys of aluminum and beryllium. The hull was ingeniously braced to enable it to withstand tremendous shocks or immense pressure. The ship carried an equipment of hydrodyne generators totaling more than five hundred thousand horsepower—an absurdly large power plant it seemed to me.

The machine had caterpillar tread for travel overland or over the ocean floor, screws for propulsion over the water, vanes and rudders for diving, and another more unusual feature—rocket tubes to drive it through air or through empty space! They were of Sam's invention, and of novel design. They were loaded with water, and contained resistance coils through which a tremendous current could be sent from the generators, heating the special metal tubes to a temperature of some thousands of degrees, and converting the water into superheated steam at enormous pressure, which, escaping at the nozzles, would propel the ship by reaction.

According to Sam's figures, the machine should be able to hurl itself a hundred miles in ten minutes, but it seemed very unlikely that it would ever be able to develop the speed of seven miles per second required to get clear of the Earth's gravitation.

Amidships, above the control cabin, was a low revolving turret, or conning tower, containing a second instrument board, so that the machine could be driven either from there or from below. It carried not only periscopes and other instruments, but a two-inch automatic cannon, of a recent design, capable of firing gas, shrapnel, or high-explosive shells at the rate of two hundred and twenty per minute. There was a small torpedo tube forward; and, as a further addition to the armament, Sam had installed transformer and projectors for using the half-million horsepower of the generators to produce a vast electric arc.

Arrangements for the life and comfort of the passengers were not lacking. There were oxygen tanks and caustic potash containers to purify the air. The walls were provided with heat insulation, and the temperature was automatically controlled by electricity. The control room below the conning tower, with the instruments at one end, was fitted up like a luxurious little library. Forward was the tiny galley and dining room, aft, a miniature stateroom. The remarkably compact generators and machinery were in a compartment in the stern. There was a space in the bow for supplies of concentrated food, spare parts for the machinery, arms and ammunitions, and miscellaneous supplies.

So fast did the building proceed that, within three months after the day of darkness, the last plane of the construction fleet was gone. We began to supply the vessel at once. Sam selected the foodstuff, and had enough put on board to last us for many years. We had a supply of ammunition for the machine gun, and an assortment of rifles and pistols. Sam had a little corner fitted up for a laboratory, and stocked with instruments and apparatus of all varieties. In the cabin I put the better part of my collection of the old romances. We were preparing a little world of our own, getting ready to be cut off from civilization, forever!

Last of all, Sam set up on board of our craft the great machine with which he had battled the strange force in the ether to bring back the sun. He had not given up. I knew that, even if he saw no hope, he would not surrender so long as he lived. He would carry on the war to the end.

As it stood on the beach below the cottage, the Omnimobile was a strange-looking machine. Gleaming like silver in the bright sunshine of those last days, it looked like a vast metal monster. It was bulky, almost clumsy looking; but it had somehow the air of an irresistible strength that could force a way through forests and surmount mountain peaks. In its resistless power, it suggested the old saurian lords of the jungle. With its low, thick body, and the massive strength of its construction, there seemed little doubt that it might go almost anywhere it chose, and be able to take care of itself upon arrival.

The last day came. For two weeks we had been ready to move aboard whenever the alien force brought the frozen night again to Earth. I had been living in it, while Sam spent most of his time in the laboratory. I whiled the time away by wandering on the beach, bathing in the surf, or dreaming idly. I tried to believe I did not care too much. I tried to think I could go on serenely, the last man alive, forgetting the dead Earth—happy in my dreams of the Green Girl!

CHAPTER SEVEN
The Globe of Crimson Doom

FOR SOME TIME I had felt that Sam was afraid of something, of a danger more personal than the freezing of the Earth. He had said little about it, but from his hints I gathered that he thought the mysterious force he was struggling against might do something to sweep him and his machine out of the way. He spent hours alone in the little room, with the apparatus that registered new force in the ether, manipulating his switches, and dials, with the phones on his ears, and his eyes fixed on the color screen, listening and watching intently—for what?

There was no man on Earth with enough knowledge of science to follow him. None could have understood his explanations, even if he had given them. So the world will never know.

It was just after sunset that the amazing thing took place that showed the full power and alertness of the incredible force that menaced the Earth. I was sitting in a folding chair on the narrow white metal deck of the machine, leaning back against the squat conning tower, with the black muzzle of the little gun sticking out over my head. I had a book in my hand, but it was closed, and I was gazing out at the sea.

Sam was still at the house, although it was past our usual suppertime. Suddenly my attention was attracted by a faint hail. I glanced toward the cottage and saw him running toward me at a desperate pace, head down and legs working like pistons.

Though I was unable to imagine what the matter might be, I got up, opened the hatch, carried down my chair and started the motors, in case he might want to move the machine. In a moment I heard him scrambling up the ladder at the side, heard his quick footsteps across the deck. He dived into the room, shouting breathlessly, "It's coming! Quick! Start—"

Before I could move, he had brushed me from the instrument board. The heavy throbbing drone of the hydrodyne units rose higher, and in an instant the Omnimobile had lunged forward, with a great rattle and clanking of metal, so suddenly that I fell against the wall.

I was amazed at the speed we developed. Sam was not sparing the machinery. The clanging roar was almost deafening. The whole machine vibrated to the engine beat, and it rolled and tossed so much that I could hardly recover my feet. With face set and expressionless, with blue eyes straight ahead, Sam stood with his hands on the levers.

He went straight up the beach, without regard for trees or fences. Suddenly he swung the wheel about in a wild attempt to avoid a shelving declivity that led down to the water. Our speed was too great. Momentum carried us on. The machine rolled over completely, tossing me about the padded conning tower like a doll. When I got up again the invincible machine was still forging on, with Sam undisturbed at the controls.

We were two miles from the cottage when he brought the Omnimobile to a standstill on the hard white sand a hundred yards above the water, and turned off the engines. With a sigh of relief he turned to face me, pulling out a red bandanna to wipe the beads of sweat from his brow. He grinned faintly.

"Rather a narrow squeak, that. I was not looking for it—so soon. We were just in time; I thought they had us!"

"But what—what is it?" I stammered, still seeing no cause for our mad flight, though I had no doubt there had been cause enough. "Who—"

"Wait and see," Sam suggested grimly. "I hadn't imagined they could do such a thing. I just happened to pick up the warning in time. Mel, the thing we're fighting must be a million years ahead of us. I never dreamed of such a thing!"

I looked out through the thick lenticular windows of the conning tower, but failed to see anything unusual.

"Get your binoculars and we'll go on deck," Sam said. "I'm sure we're out of danger here."

I was not so sure about that, but I got the heavy glasses, and we stepped out on the metal deck. I looked back in the direction of the place whence we had come. The world was very still. Even the sea was almost silent. The old cottage on the hill behind us seemed suddenly very desolate and lonely, standing out, a solitary dark point, against the dying glow of the westward sky. It seemed very bleak and ancient.

And then I saw a curious thing—an astonishing thing. There was something *bright* hanging in the air a hundred yards above the building—something that shone with a silvery gleam! Steadily it grew brighter against the dull, somber curtain of the darkling western sky. Then I saw that it was a huge globe of white, metallic light. It was a great gleaming silver ball, evidently many feet in diameter. It glowed with a queer, unnatural effulgence. It was like a little floating moon!

In a moment I saw that a faint greenish haze was gathering about it. With astonishing swiftness a veil of glowing green mist was drawn about the sphere of shining white. It became a vast luminous green cloud that swirled and shifted in thin, feathery streamers, drawn around the shining central globe. It swam, and swirled, and grew! It wheeled madly, dizzily, ever reaching out. It was a mist of flame like the photosphere about the sun. A strange, weird light shone from it, lighting the sea and the beach and the woodland about the doomed building with an uncanny radiance!

Quite abruptly two narrow beams of a thick, misty purple fire darted out of the silver core of the amazing thing, and, flashing over the ground, fixed themselves upon the cottage! They were like thin, unpleasant fingers of purple fog. There was something terrible in the swift sureness of their motions. They moved as if were seeing eyes, or tentacles—feeling, searching!

Suddenly they were gone. In a moment I noted a change. The seething clouds of green were sucked down. They drew into a dense cyclonic vortex of flame about the old house, like a falling torrent of molten emerald. The building was half hidden in the thick, racing fog. I strained my ears, but not a sound did I hear, save the soft whisper of the sea. The cloak of green mist swirled about its core with a silence that was complete—and terrible!

Suddenly the ancient house burst into strange red incandescence. The chimney, gables and corners shone with a dull, lurid scarlet fire. There was no flame, just a dusky, crimson gleam. It grew brighter and deeper, until it was an intense, bloody glare. And then the climbing vines and trees about it, gleaming like ruby plants, began to melt away! The house began to dissolve into crimson light!

The green mist swirled lower. The silvery central moon waxed brighter. Once or twice thin fingers of purple mist were again thrust out exploringly, all in a silence of death. And the red gleam grew! The house glowed as though washed in a rain of blood. And swiftly it faded into that awful light!

The chimney tottered and came down in a shower of red sparks that faded into nothingness before they touched the ground. The roof fell, and the remnant of the walls collapsed upon it in a heap of crimson dust of fire that faded swiftly— dissolved—vanished!

The little hill was a bare red waste, gleaming with that terrible scarlet glare. The two purple tentacles of misty flame shot out again, and swept searchingly over the spot. Suddenly the green mist stopped its seething motion. Its fires died out. It grew dim, faded, and was gone like a cloud of dissipating steam. The white glow of the silver globe waxed dull, and suddenly it, too, was no more.

Quickly the red glow faded from the weirdly denuded hilltop and the night fell in a heavy mantle. I stood wrapt in a spell of amazement and terror.

CHAPTER EIGHT
Out of the Sea's Abyss

"WELL, HOW was the show?" Sam's voice was a little weak and strained. Suddenly I was conscious of an unpleasant tremor of the knees. I went into the conning tower and dropped myself weakly on a seat. I tried to speak, but my mouth was very dry. I swallowed twice.

"What was it?" I contrived to articulate at last.

The old man stood erect in the opening, with a hand upon his thoughtful brow. "I don't know," he said. "I didn't think they could come. They must have mastered secrets of time and space that we know nothing of. They have conquered our limitations of distance. They must be ages ahead of us!"

"But the house—it just melted away!"

"As for that, the emanations of the green cloud must have disrupted the atoms, allowing the electrons to fall together to make neutrons (formed of united protons and electrons) so small that they fell through the ground, toward the center of the Earth. That is easy enough to understand—in fact, I could probably have developed a similar ray myself, as a result of my work on the hydrodyne. The strange thing is how they got here!"

"The thing just seemed to appear and vanish!"

"Possibly we could see it only when it was lit with the radiation of the green. It may have just slipped up and away in the darkness. But it is more likely—judging from the etheric disturbance it created—that it did not come through our space at all, but moved by the distortion of hyper-space—came through the fourth dimension, in effect!"

"And they seemed to know just where to strike."

"Yes. They must have found that by triangulation on my interference waves I was doing the same trick for them when the apparatus warned me."

"You were what?"

"I have been working a long time to get the direction of that mysterious force."

"And you succeeded?"

"You remember the Mangar Deep?"

"What? Oh, yes. Discovered in the South Pacific by Mangar and Kane about 1945."

"In 1946, I believe. The disturbance comes from there. *It emanates from a point ten miles below the level of the Pacific!*"

"What? Impossible!"

"Do I make mistakes?" Sam asked softly.

"No. But the discoverers reported only six miles of water. And anyhow, men couldn't live under there."

"The exact spot is somewhat south of their soundings. But, Mel, don't assume that we have to deal with men. We may be dealing with entities that developed in the sea, even with creatures of the rocks below the sea. I tell you, it's outside the range of your old anthropomorphic fiction."

I could say nothing more. I sat still, with rather unpleasant thoughts. Intelligences that could reach casually from a point ten miles below sea level, to wipe out a building ten thousand miles away! Such things are very good in amazing romances, but extremely hard to face squarely in real life.

For many minutes Sam was silent. He had pulled out his battered pipe and filled it absently with illegal tobacco. He stood puffing on it steadily, with the dim glow coming and going on his tanned face as he drew. Presently he spoke very softly:

"Mel, we can go in the Omnimobile to see about it."

"Dive into the Deep?"

"We could do it."

"Ten miles of water. Good Lord! That would crush us like—like—"

"I think the machine would stand it."

"But what could we do?"

"We don't know until we know what needs to be done."

"It means death." I whispered hoarsely. "And the Green Girl. When I am dead I may dream of her no more. It may be that she lives only in my mind, and when I die—"

Sam said nothing. He merely waited, puffing away, with his pipe smoke drifting out into the night. In a moment I had considered, and realized my selfishness. I thrust out my hand, and he gripped it firmly.

"I knew you would see it, Mel," he cried with a glad ring in his voice. "Whoever, and whatever they are, they haven't got us yet. We're still kicking!"

"We start for the Mangar Deep—"

"—At sunrise in the morning."

We climbed down into the machine, and went together into the galley to fix supper. Sam got out his old music box and played through his ancient favorite selections, and then we went to our miniature staterooms. But I did not sleep soon that night. The Green Girl came to me in a fresh and vivid waking dream. She was, as ever, supremely, superbly beautiful, with dark curls, smiling red lips; and clear, sparkling violet eyes. I told her of the struggle I had had, and that I was resolved to set out upon the fateful cruise. And she seemed very happy, so I regretted my decision no longer. So, very happy, I fell asleep, and had dreams of the Green Girl that were dreams indeed.

At dawn I was awakened by the rattle of pots and pans in the galley. I sprang out of my bunk, took an icy shower, and ran into the dining room where Sam had breakfast ready. The stores had been well selected, and Sam was a prince among chefs. Whatever our fate, we would approach it feasting like kings.

He seemed as cheerful and confident as myself. Now that the issue was determined, the uncertainty of action was removed, and we both felt oddly relieved. After we had eaten, we started the engines and drove the machine back to the hilltop where the cottage had been. We got out and examined the surface of the ground that had been acted upon by the strange red dissolution.

The earth had evidently been eaten away to a depth of several feet, and the surface was left covered with a hard, greenish vitrified crust, smooth and hard as glass. It was unpleasant to think what would have happened if Sam had failed to intercept the warning of the approach of that amazing machine—if it had been a machine.

CHAPTER NINE
Into the Mangar Deep

WE HURRIED BACK into the Omnimobile; climbed into the conning tower, and started the engines again. Sam turned the bow toward the sea, and the great machine crawled slowly down to meet the lapping white waves. In a few moments they were slapping and splashing against her sides.

On we drove, down the sloping sand. The green water rose about the windows. In a moment the periscope screen showed that we were entirely under water. We crawled steadily over the bottom of the sea, deeper and deeper. All the wonders of the hidden sea-life lay about us, bright corals and strange shrubs, curious rocks, and beautiful dells between them, through which silvery fishes and stranger monsters of the deep were moving. It grew darker, and Sam turned on the powerful searchlights. We moved on down into stranger regions. But I must not take space for that, for we were hastening toward a world that was weirder by far!

In half an hour we closed the valves, which had been left open to let the water flood the tanks, and started the pumps. We were lifted above the ocean floor. We stopped the caterpillar tread, and set the screws into motion. In a few minutes the Omnimobile rose above the surface and splashed back into the blue waves like a gigantic dolphin of silver metal!

I climbed out on the deck. The Florida coast was a bright green line in the west. The serene blue vault of the heavens was illimitable above us, and the deeper blue expanse of waters lay about in a flat, measureless plain. The machine throbbed almost imperceptibly with the motors, and the prow sent out two white wings of water. The plates were wet and slippery with the spray. I thrilled to feel again the motion of a powerful craft beneath me, to smell the salty tang of the air, and to feel the tingle of the salt mist upon my skin. We were making a good fifty knots, and I had to brace myself against the cool, damp wind of our progress. Thanks to her gyrostabilizers, the vessel was perfectly steady.

I stood there a long time, gripping the low rail, and lost in the wonders of sea and sky. I felt very much a part of all that splendid, sunlit world. I felt a deep, poignant regret at leaving it. But I found myself feeling—with a little surprise—that I could be willing enough to give up my life to save it!

At last I went back into the conning tower. Sam stood alert at the controls, with an odd, exultant light in his eyes, and with a smile of joy and confidence on his lean face. With his hands on the levers, he turned to me and said:

"The little old machine's a wonder, Mel. She runs on sea, land, or air! It's a great feeling to drive her. She'd go anywhere. You know, I wish we had time to make a trial for the moon!"

"There's no hurry about that," I assured him heartily. "The moon will keep."

Presently I took the controls. Sam fixed dinner, and brought my meal in on a tray. Then he went to his stateroom. I enjoyed my spell at the controls. Indeed, as Sam had said, the handling of the machine gave one a strange sensation of power, of omnipotence, almost. It was the same feeling of unconquerable, careless power that a god might have enjoyed. I was almost sorry when Sam came to relieve me in the evening, and I had to go I to my bunk.

When I got up to take his place again, it was night. The generators were beating steadily, and the Omnimobile was ploughing her way through heavy seas. The sky was black, and occasional brilliant flashes of lightning lit the sheets of falling rain that drummed on the metal deck. When he showed me our position, it was in the Pacific, off Central America. I knew that he had used the rocket tubes to carry us over the Isthmus. For two more days we kept the bow southwest, in the direction of the Mangar Deep. Sam and I alternated at the controls, and he took time to prepare our meals when he was off duty.

The cabin was fixed up most comfortably with bookcases, table, and upholstered divan. During the second long afternoon I looked over my old stories of science, and read again Verne's immortal story, *Twenty Thousand Leagues Under the Sea*. I was somewhat amused at the thought that I was aboard a stranger and more wonderful machine than that of the fantastic tale, and that our adventures had already been far more amazing than those of the great romance at which so many practical people had scoffed. If I had known what was to come—well, I suppose I could not have composed myself enough to read at all!

At evening on the third day, the sea lay cold and blue about us, and the northern sun was crawling along the horizon to sink cold and bright in the clear northwestern sky, turning the westward waves into a glittering sea of frozen fire, and gleaming with prismatic whiteness on the snow caps of a few vast icebergs that dotted that far southern sea. Sam stopped the engines. We floated in that wintry, lonely ocean, infinitely removed from the busy world of man, over the Mangar Deep—over the lair of the hidden menace!

I stood on the gleaming wet metal deck, shivering slightly from the chill of the keen south wind, breathing deep of the fresh salty air, and lost in the never-aging wonders of the sea and sky. I felt even a distant kinship with the blue, white-capped mountains of ice that lifted their massive frozen spires to meet the cold sunshine. How often, in the incredible adventure to come, was I to fear that I was never again to see the blue of the sky, or to feel the ancient spell of a limitless surging sea.

I took a last deep breath, and went below. I was a little surprised to see that Sam was closing the ventilators, opening the oxygen apparatus and air purifiers, inspecting the pumps and valves, getting ready to dive.

"Surely we can't start till morning?"

"Why not? At two hundred fathoms night is the same as day."

"I hadn't thought of that. Then—"

"Before we see the sky again, we shall know—"

With a queer tightening in my throat, I saw the manhole closed for the last time upon the fresh, cold air of the sea. In ten minutes more we had let the water into the buoyancy tanks. Green water and gleaming monsters of the sea rushed upward in the steady glare of the searchlights beyond the windows.

I stood at the valve and pump controls, while Sam busied himself in seeing to the torpedo tube and the machine gun, and in adjusting his electric arc weapon. Then he brought out a grotesque suit of steel submarine armor he had had made, with oxygen tanks and electric searchlight, etc., attached.

Swiftly we were dropping into the Mangar Deep!

CHAPTER TEN
The Depths of Fear

IN THE DEEP SEA the temperature is just above freezing; the darkness is absolute; the pressure is many tons to the square inch. But still, life has been found, even in the greatest depths. It is strange life, to be sure, for the organisms must be developed to withstand the great pressure, and to generate their own light. It is an odd truth of nature that there is some form of life adapted for each locality. There are the mosses and reindeer of the frigid north, the cactus and lizards of the burning deserts, the blind creatures of the Mammoth Cave, the stranger things of the deepest seas. May it not be that there are entities living out in space, or in the Earth's interior, of which we may never know? Such were my thoughts as we dropped to meet the menace that had risen from under the sea.

We sank swiftly, and steadily the manometer climbed. The water was dark but for the bright beams of the searchlights, and very cold, though, with the insulation and the electric heaters, we felt no discomfort. The pressure on the plates must have been terrific beyond conception. It seemed impossible that metal—even our cleverly braced plates of the wonderful beryllium bronze—could withstand so much, when even the rocks of the ocean floor "creep" and bend beneath the water's weight!

Thousands upon thousands of feet we sank, and still the sea was dark and cold. In our wild plunge downward I caught fleeting glimpses of many of the weirdly grotesque creatures of the deep, flashing past in the gleam of our lights.

At last Sam had completed his preparations for the emergency that might arise when we reached our goal. He came into the conning tower. I looked at the manometer—in fact, I had been looking at it most of the time.

"Pressure four thousand pounds!" I read. "That means we are nearly eight thousand feet down. I wonder how much longer—"

"Remember," Sam said softly. "Remember that we have to go ten miles down—fifty-thousand feet."

"Fifty-thousand feet! Every cubic foot of water weighs sixty-five pounds. Fifty thousand times sixty-five, divided over one hundred and forty-four square inches. That is— about twenty-two thousand pounds to the square inch. Eleven tons!"

"Somewhat more, I fancy, say 23,800 pounds," Sam observed calmly.

"What's the difference? Nothing could live or move under such a weight."

"The thing we have come to investigate lives there, if it is a living thing at all."

I said nothing more. Somehow, I did not feel inclined to conversation. I could think only of the terrific weight of water so near, pressing so mercilessly upon the thin plates, think only of how cruelly it would crush and tear us when it found its way in! I gazed at the little needle with a sort of fascination. It crept slowly around the dial, counting up the pounds of the irresistible pressure that surrounded us.

The minutes dragged by. The little needle showed a depth of fifteen thousand feet, almost three miles. The height of a good mountain, and still it crept up! And yet we were not a third of the way. Suddenly I heard a splintering crackle that grated roughly on my strained nerves. I looked down. The unconscious grip of my hand had splintered the top panel of the back of a chair by my side!

Sam was looking at me, grinning. "I'm glad you didn't have your hand on me, Mel."

I glanced back at the needle, and shouted in surprised relief.

"It has stopped!"

Truly, the pointer stood still. As we watched it, it hung still a moment under my riveted gaze, and then crept back!

"It's a turning point. The pressure is getting less!"

"It couldn't be!" Sam said. "Unless we are rising."

"No! See—the buoyancy tanks are still flooded!"

"The duplicate pressure gauge?"

"It turned back with the other."

"Look! Yes, we are still sinking." He pointed to the windows.

"See—the fish are still flashing upward in the light."

In speechless wonder, we stood and watched. Still we were evidently sinking. Still the dark waters rushed up about us. And still the needles crept back!

Suddenly Sam seized my shoulder in a hand of iron. "Look!" he whispered hoarsely, pointing out through the heavy lenses. "Can't you see? A light! A red gleam beyond our searchlights!"

A switch clicked under the nervous fingers of his other hand, and our lights went out. In a moment, as soon as my eyes were accustomed to the darkness, I saw that he was right. The sea was not black! There was a pale, roseate glow suffused through it.

Steadily it grew stronger. We were coming into a region of light, and of decreased pressure, at the bottom of the sea. Of all wonders!

The red light grew stronger, until it seemed that we sank through a sea of molten ruby—through an ocean of blood. Intense red light poured in through the lenses until I had to hide my eyes. With shaded eyes, Sam bent over the manometer.

"Only two hundred feet!" he cried. "Fifty! Ten!"

Suddenly the floor fell away from beneath my feet. We seemed to have dropped from the sea into a lake of fire. A blindingly intense red glare poured in the windows. I was very sick. The ship reeled about me, the floor sank, dropped away! I grasped dizzily for the table, drew myself blindly toward it.

I remember hanging limply and helplessly to the table for a moment, remember Sam pushing me suddenly away. I have a dim memory of a crashing thunder of sound that reverberated deafeningly and seemed to roll away to infinite distances through the fiery mist. And with that strange, deep sound, my consciousness faded away!

CHAPTER ELEVEN
The Roof of Waters

THE NEXT THING I knew I was lying on the floor with a torrent of icy water falling on my face. I sat up, sputtering. Sam was bending over me with a relieved grin on his face.

"Care for any more?" he asked, emptying the pail.

"That's quite enough, thanks," I sputtered. "Where are we?"

"Right here."

"Talk sense," I pleaded, trying to get up, and rubbing the bump in my head.

"Really, I hardly know," he said, soberly. "It's rather queer. We're afloat on a smooth, warm sea. The sky is red!"

I stared at him stupidly.

"It's a good thing we had the rockets. If we hadn't used them, we'd have hit this water like a concrete pavement."

"Queer, you say. My eye! We're both crazy! It can't be!"

"You might get up and see for yourself."

"You say we've fallen through the Pacific and into another sea?"

"I only know what I can see."

"We did seem to come out of the water into a red mist."

"So it seemed."

"But the Pacific Ocean overhead! We must have come through six miles of water. And water won't float on air."

"We have several interesting questions before us."

I got uncertainly to my feet, walked past the calm old scientist, and climbed out on the narrow deck. Indeed it was a weird and incredible sight that met my eyes. Overhead arched a great dome of crimson fire. In all directions it reached down to the dark, warm sea on which we were floating. Nothing in sight but red sky and dark waves! There was a light, hot breeze, but the strange sea was very still. Its color was a blue-black, splashed weirdly with the reflected light of the crimson sky. It stretched out on every hand to where the red sky rose, utterly lifeless—lonely and dead.

We had fallen into an unsuspected and incredible world!

Miles of water lay between us and our fellow men. Suddenly I felt an absurdly great loneliness, a vast homesickness for the world we had left—even if my fellow men had never meant very much to me! I felt an ineffably intense desire for the sunshine, for blue skies and green plains, and for the busy, cheerful cities of men. In fact, I almost burst into tears.

It was not so much that I was afraid. But the place seemed so strange that even after I was dead my soul could not find a way out!

If there had been a rock, or an island to break the monotony of the ghostly, silent sea, it would not have been so bad. But there were none. The strange dark desert of waters stretched out as far as my eye could reach. The eerie, scarlet radiation of the sky beat down with intense heat, and the wind was damp and sultry.

Abruptly Sam stepped out beside me. There was almost a grin on his lean, tanned face, and he looked somehow very confident and resourceful. I felt a great wave of faith in him and in the wonderful machine beneath our feet, reeking silently in the strange, smooth sea. Impulsively I reached out my hand to him, and he took it with a smile.

"I know how you feel, Mel. But we're still kicking!"

"But the ocean?" I asked again. "What could hold it up?"

"I've been doing some pretty stiff thinking along that line. I have a theory that might help you, even if I have missed the point. You know we came through the red gas that makes the curious sky we see. The gas was just below the water. It's evidently radioactive, or it wouldn't be luminous. Its emanations might change the gravity of the water above!"

"Negative gravity or levitation?"

"Something of the kind. You know that science has held for a long time that there is no reason, *per se,* to doubt the existence of substances that would repel instead of attracting one another. In fact, the mutual repulsion of the like poles of a magnet is, in a way, an illustration of that very thing. Even assuming the existence of substances of negative gravity, they would not be found on the surface of the Earth, for they would escape into space as fast as liberated. The phlogiston of the old alchemists, by the way, was supposed to be such a substance.

"But suppose the gravity of the water is negative by the gas. Water, you know, has the property of becoming radioactive after it has been exposed to radium emanations, and it is logical enough for it to assume the qualities of the gas. The water next to the gas may support that above."

"But it looks as if the gas would bubble out, like air under water," I said.

"That was the principal objection to the theory. But we know from our pressure readings that the water is not resting heavily on the gas. If it is supported by the negative gravity of its lower stratum, the equilibrium is very delicate, but it would be naturally maintained.

"Suppose the roof of water is lifted. The gas and atmosphere below, being given more room, would expand. Consequently the gas would be brought less intimately into contact with the water, the negativing effect would be reduced, and the balance would be restored. Conversely, a sinking would compress the gas, increase its effect, and bring back the balance. Even if the water sank in one place and was lifted in another, the difference in the density of the gas at various altitudes would maintain the equilibrium."

"Yes. Yes, I believe I see. A thousand thanks! It makes me feel a lot better to see how it could be," I said, admiring the wonderful readiness with which he had formulated his theory. "But can you say how the gas came to be here, and how there happens to be breathable air beneath it?"

"Both might have been manufactured by the intelligences we have come to investigate. More likely, however, the gas comes from the disintegration of the radium in the Earth, and has been rising out of fissures in the ocean floor and collecting here for ages. The oxygen of the air may have come from the decomposition of rocks—the Earth's crust is almost fifty percent oxygen. This place may be as old as the sea. That alien power may have been growing up in here through all the ages that man has been developing outside!"

"You think there may be living things here?"

"No reason why not. In fact, this is the logical habitat for your Green Girl. Red and green are complementary colors. If there are people here, green would be the natural color for the protective pigmentation against this red light."

CHAPTER TWELVE
The Second Sea

LEAVING ME to the visions and the flights of wild hope that his last words induced, Sam went below. In a few minutes he called me to eat. Suddenly I realized that I was very hungry. I looked at my watch. It was eight o'clock.

"Why, is it just two hours since we left the surface?"

"No. It's fourteen!"

Forgetting the intense red sky, the strange, smooth sea, and the damp, hot wind, I went below to meet Sam's wonderful biscuit, with fresh steak and fruit from the refrigerator. A very mild and colorless beginning for adventurers newly fallen into an unknown world, but a very sensible one!

After the meal, each of us took a turn on guard in the conning tower, while the other slept. Nothing happened. The soft hot wind blew steadily out of the south, the bloody glare of the weird sky was changeless, and the sea lay about in a motionless desert.

The thermometer outside registered 115°, but on account of the automatic temperature control, the machine was comfortable enough, though the heat and humidity on deck were stifling.

When we had rested, we turned the bow of the Omnimobile toward the north and cruised along at a speed of four or five knots. I stood in the conning tower at the wheel, while Sam busied himself with making an analysis of the air, and of a sample of water from the sea. Presently he came up out of the little laboratory, with his report.

"The air shows to be 31% oxygen," he said, "and 64% helium, with the remainder a mixture of various other gases. The barometer pressure is only eleven pounds, which compensates for the excess of oxygen. The helium is a good indication of the radioactivity that must have produced the gas overhead, since helium is one of the ultimate products of radium disintegration. The oxygen must have come largely from the breaking up of carbon dioxide by plant life."

"Then there is life?"

"There were microscopic organisms, both animal and vegetable, in the sample of water I took. The water, by the way, carries only 1.23% solid matter, mostly sodium chloride. Less than half as much as the sea above, which has 2.7%."

For several hours longer we moved slowly over the surface of that warm, silent sea. In all directions it lay flat as far as my eye could reach, its blue-black depths glancing with the unearthly crimson of the sky. Sam was still working in the laboratory and looking after the machinery.

And then I saw the first living thing!

My roving eye caught a tiny black speck against the gleam of the bloody sky. It was soaring, drifting slowly, like a vast bird—its motion was too irregular, I thought, to be that of a flying machine. I flung the little port open, and tried to get my binoculars upon it. It was very far away, but I made out that it was a vast, strange, winged thing. It seemed very large to be a bird. And its colors were bright—fantastic! It seemed—I was sure—that its wings were green! But it seemed to be moving faster than I had thought. I never got it clearly into focus, and suddenly it dived, and was lost beneath the horizon.

"Sam! Sam!" I called sharply. "I've seen something— something *alive!*"

In a moment he was climbing up into the conning tower, with a question on his lips. I described my confused impression of the thing as best I could, mentioning the strange colors.

"More than likely, Mel," he said, "you wouldn't have recognized it, even if you had seen it clearly. You could hardly expect to find life here like that we know. The chances are that evolution has taken a widely different course in here. Even the tiny things in the sea were strange to me. And in a world like this, of hot and endless day, we're likely to find jungles with great insects and huge reptiles—a fauna and flora corresponding to that of the Carboniferous Era on the surface."

"Then you think there is land here, trees, even men! You really think—the Green Girl?"

"That was just an idea, about the green tan. But there is sure to be land, of some sort, where the lips of this abyss curve up to meet the water above. And there is no reason why there might not be life upon it—highly developed life, at that. Life may be as old in this place as outside, perhaps older, for it has been protected from the cataclysms of one kind and another that may have swept life off the surface again and again through the ages. And we know there is some kind of intelligence here—"

"No wonder they were willing to freeze the Earth! They couldn't tell the difference if the sea were frozen a mile thick!"

Still we held our course to the northward. Presently Sam went back below again. An hour later the horizon was broken by a line of dull blue in the north. A thin blue strip appeared between black sea and scarlet sky, and widened slowly. In another hour I could make out a wall of towering blue cliffs all across the north, rising from the sea as if to support the red sky. They were veiled in the mists of infinite distances. When Sam had made his observations, computed his angles and completed his calculations, he announced that they were a hundred miles north of us, and met the red sky at a level four miles above us as we floated along!

That meant that we were nine miles below the level of the Pacific, according to Sam's figures. The seat of the menace we thought to conquer was a mile below us yet!

As the hours went by, and we still went northward at our crawling pace (we went slowly because Sam thought that the use of the engines at full power would create an etheric disturbance that would reveal our position to our mysterious enemy). The jagged rim of the abyss rose steadily out of the sea. The cliffs, when I focused my powerful glasses upon them, seemed composed of sheer columns of blue rock, reaching up to meet the red roof of waters like gigantic prisms of blue basalt.

At last my searching eyes glimpsed a patch of green below the blue. A vast slope of green hills drew up out of the red-black sea. They gleamed with the pure verdant emerald of well-watered grasslands. Here and there they were marked with huge, strange splotches of purple. I was ever amazed anew at the vastness of the weird world about us.

Steadily the green and purple slopes lifted themselves out of the dark sea before us, and stretched up, through vast plains and low hills, to the sheer wall of rough blue cliffs that lay all about the north, cut off so sharply at the top by the red sky.

At last we came in view of the shore—fringed with a vast jungle of green and lofty forest. Huge those many strange plants were, with long thick leaves, grotesque forms, and fantastic flaming blossoms! I stared intently at them through the binoculars. They were like nothing that is or has ever been above the sea—like nothing that I had ever seen or imagined! They were strange wild trees of another Earth! Their green was weirdly tinted with purple, or with queer metallic tints of silver and bronze! Their incredibly great blooms were prolifically borne and infinitely varied, making the weird jungle an alien fairyland of bright and multicolored flame.

A fit habitat, indeed, for the monstrous things we found there!

CHAPTER THIRTEEN
The Flying Flowers

IT WAS SEVERAL MILES back of the shore to where the green grassland rose from the jungle to slope up to the cliffs of gleaming blue. I had ceaselessly searched the plains and the jungles for a sign of life or intelligence; but, so far, I had seen nothing save the weird flying monster of which I had caught a glimpse.

But suddenly a huge winged thing arose from the jungle strip! In a moment two more had joined it from the shore! In a few minutes a score of vast weird monsters were circling over the beach ahead. They were strange things, incredible, almost. I might have doubted my eyes but for Sam's warning of the strange things we might encounter. Their colors were bright. The wings were plainly green and of a spread of many yards! They flew with slow and regular wing-beats.

It was some time before I got one focused clearly in the glasses and then I gasped in astonishment and terror at the weird creature that seemed to spring at me from the lenses. It was neither bird nor winged reptile. It was not an animal at all.

It was a winged plant!

The great flapping wings were broad and green, braced with white veins like the leaf of a plant. The long body was plated with coarse brown scales, and tapered to a green-fringed tail. Eight long blood-red tentacles dangled in pairs below the body. They were thick, and the coils of each must have measured many yards in length. Each bore at the end a single terrible claw. *And instead of a head, the thing carried on the forward end—a flower!* It was huge, of many petals, brightly colored! Out of the calyx were thrust three dead-black, knobbed appendages that must have been organs of sense.

It was a vast thing—unbelievable! It was as large as an airplane. It was terrible—a nightmare monster! I could scarcely believe my sight, though, after what Sam had said, I might have expected such a thing.

I do not remember calling Sam. I was too much amazed. But suddenly he climbed up beside me, and took the binoculars from my unconscious hand. With a fearful gaze, I watched him raise and focus the instrument, trying to read in his lean, tanned face the meaning of the astounding things.

I saw keen interest reflected there, surprise, intense concentration, but nothing of the strange terror I felt. A sensation of immense relief came over me, and I made a half-hearted effort to smile as he lowered the glasses and looked at me, grinning.

"Don't let it get you, Mel," he said. "I was expecting something of the sort—or more so. They are no more terrible than the old winged saurians, probably. At any rate, the Omnimobile can take care of herself. We're likely to meet something worse before we're through."

"I hope not!" I said, piously. "But the things are plants!"

"Possibly. But the idea of animated plants is nothing new to science. The line of division between the plant and animal kingdoms is rather vague, and it seems that both developed from a common ancestor. Even today there are living things that can be classified neither as plant nor animal. Take, for instance, *Euglena Viridis,* the microscopic organism that colors green scum on fresh-water ponds. It is a plant, because it contains chlorophyll, and utilizes sunlight in the manufacture of food from carbon dioxide and it absorbs salts dissolved in the water. It is an animal because it can swim about very actively, and because it can absorb particles of food that it finds in the water. Carry the evolution of such a thing to the nth degree, and you have the flying things before us!"

Again, I had to admit that Sam had advanced a most plausible explanation for an amazing thing, but still I prefer my plants fastened to the ground.

It soon became evident that the monsters had discovered us. They approached and circled close above, green wings slowly beating the air, and the great blooms that were like heads seeming to flicker with varied colors: The thick, red tentacles coiled below the great brown shark-like bodies, with terrible talons drawn back threateningly.

"The things may be feeling unpleasant," Sam suggested. "It might be a good thing to fix 'em a hot welcome."

That had already occurred to me. I let Sam have the controls, and ran out and loaded the little cannon. Through the thick windows of the little conning tower I watched the monsters flying above us. They followed as we kept up our deliberate advance toward the jungle-covered shore.

Suddenly one of them dived down upon us. The impact of its heavy, shark-like body shook the machine, and its great claws grated over the metal plates with an unpleasantly suggestive sound, as it strove vainly to rip them open. I felt some alarm. For sheer fighting power I would match one of those flying plants against any animal that ever walked on Earth. In wing spread it was fully as long as the Omnimobile, though the machine was, of course, many times heavier.

I slipped into gear the machinery that revolved the turret, and as soon as a portion of that rough, armored brown body was fairly before the gun, I let fire with an explosive shell. The whole machine rocked with the force of the explosion, and the side of that vast scaly brown body was torn off. A viscid green fluid gushed out, dying the deck and tinting the water alongside. The terrible grasp of the thing relaxed, and it slipped off into the sea.

The others were hovering low, but in a moment Sam had submerged the machine, and we made for the shore under water. In five minutes we struck a soft, muddy bank. He shifted the caterpillar tread into gear. The machine waddled up the muddy slope through the fringe of strange plants, and broke into the weird jungle.

The unearthly radiance of the sky filtered through the jungle roof in a dull crimson light. In the vague, ominous twilight, huge and monstrous tree-trunks rose all about us, as much like great fungoid growths as like normal trees. We pushed through thickets of weird purples and strange metallic hues, under vast masses of hanging green vines, all hung with gigantic incredible blooms that were so bright they seemed to light the dusky forest with their vivid flames of crimson and yellow and blue!

For perhaps three miles the Omnimobile smashed her deliberate way like a gigantic reptilian monster through that strip of weird rotting jungle. Then we emerged on higher ground of a different vegetation.

CHAPTER FOURTEEN
The Prey of the Plant

WE STOPPED the machine on the first little eminence of the open space, to survey the vastly different and unfamiliar region that lay before us. It was an open, park-like country. There were broad meadows and low hills covered with a fine turf of luxuriant green grass. There were scattering small groves and great solitary trees so profusely laden with vast purple blossoms that they seemed afire with purple flame.

It was a strange landscape, and not without a certain unearthly beauty. The rich, green plains and hills lay all about before us, scattered with clumps of brilliant purple woodland, and stretching up to the great blue cliffs in the misty distance. A lurid, melancholy weirdness was given to the scene by the awful scarlet glare of the sky.

Presently we rolled on again, across the broad level meadow, and over a little stream, and through a copse of flaming purple trees. We had gone another mile when Sam, still at the controls, shouted above the beating of the engine and the clatter of the machinery.

"Look, Mel! Get it! Shoot! North of us!"

Still behind the gun, I looked out quickly. To the north was an open green field of several acres extent. Beyond, the scattering purple trees rose, dotting the green hills until at last they merged in the slope that reached up to the cliffs in the misty distance beneath the amazing sky.

For a moment my eyes searched that strange scene in vain, and then I saw the huge green wings of one of the terrible flying plants, flapping deliberately above the brilliantly purple trees a hundred yards to our right. Sam was already swinging the machine about in that direction. Without waiting to see the cause of his frantic appeal, I trained the gun and depressed the firing pin.

The little gun roared sharply, slid quickly back and forward again in its recoil cylinders, and the mechanism clicked smoothly as another shell was thrown into the breech. For a moment my vision was obscured by the thick white cloud of smoke. Peering intently, I saw the unearthly monster flying more slowly sinking. In a moment it was out of sight behind the purple trees.

"Did you hit it?" Sam cried anxiously.

"I think so. But why all the fuss about that one? There are plenty more back in the jungle."

"Oh, didn't you see? It was carrying something!"

"Carrying something?"

"Mel, one of those red tentacles was wrapped around a *man!*"

He had brought the lumbering machine about in the direction of the place where we had last seen the monster. We went at a reckless pace. The machine rocked and banged, and we were shaken up unmercifully when we crossed a dry watercourse. Two or three of the trees went down before our undeviating and irresistible advance, filling the air with purple clouds of petals from the great bright flowers.

Then I saw before us, thirty yards away, the great strange creature lying flat on the ground with wings outspread. Beneath it, in the coils of one of the thick tentacles, I saw the gleam of a naked human body.

The machine jerked to a halt and I threw open the manhole and sprang out on the deck. In a moment Sam was beside me. He had buckled on an automatic pistol of the latest design and the heaviest caliber. He handed me a duplicate weapon, with ammunition belt and holster, with the warning, "We've got to expect the unexpected, and must be quick on the draw…"

I fastened on the gun, and led the way down the ladder to the ground. In a few seconds we stood by the dead monster. Seen at close range, it was an appalling thing, indeed. It was very strange, and even the dead body of it showed cruel strength. The green wings were like tough green leather stretched over a metal frame. The body was armored with thick, rough brown scales. The tough scarlet skin of the tentacular limbs was smooth and rubber-like. Already the weird flower at the forward end was withered and black. The ground about the thing was stained with a flood of green liquid from the terrible wound the shell had torn.

I hurried around it. Only the shoulder and arm of the human prey were in sight. Yes, it was a human being, and the skin had the clear smoothness of youth. I bent closer and perceived, with an odd admixture of feelings that made my heart beat wildly and then pause until I reeled, that the skin had a soft greenish tan. I saw that the body, lying under the wing alone, had not been crushed by the fall of the monster.

"We'll be able to tell what manner of mankind we have to deal with here," Sam said, though I scarcely heard him. "If our man was at all civilized, there ought to be ornaments, or remnants of clothing. I hardly expected human life here. But it may be a human science that is threatening our world..."

He stumbled over the end of one of the thick red tentacles. It moved uncertainly, and he stopped in a sort of fascinated horror. "God!" he muttered. Indeed, it was a terrible thing. The slick red limb, four inches thick, ended in a suction cup, with a hideous claw, a good twelve inches long, fastened at the side. It made one's flesh creep to think of that terrible claw ripping and tearing flesh, or of the cupped end of the tube sucking blood from it.

I pulled at the still white form beneath the wing. One of the crimson tentacles still clung closely about the young body. I tried to pull it free; but at my touch it seemed to tighten with a sort of aimless reflex action. Sam got out his sheath knife and cut at it. It was very tough, and the viscid green slime flowed from the abrasions in its rubber-like membrane, but presently we cut it in two. I drew the body from under the wing.

I echoed Sam's exclamation. "It's the body of a woman!"

CHAPTER FIFTEEN
The Green Girl

IT WAS, INDEED, the form of a woman—rather, of a girl. The eyelids were closed and still. There was no breathing, and no perceptible beating of the heart. But the body was very beautiful. The hair was soft and dark; the skin, white with just a hint of the green coloration. The features were regular, classic—perfect! The lips were still very red.

That form was familiar to me—it was the dearest shape of my dreams. It was the Green Girl! There could be no mistake. This was the flesh and blood reality of the delightful vision that had been the joy of my life. At last, my supreme wish was granted. I had found the Green Girl! But too late. She was so white and still.

As Sam remarked, his words reaching me faintly through a gray daze of despair, she seemed to have belonged to a rather highly developed race of people. In fact, so far as physical perfection goes, she was without parallel; and physical and mental endowments usually go hand in hand. The wide white forehead betokened a keen intellect.

Sam had expected to find ornaments on the body, but no such things as we did find. There was a thin band of metal about the waist. The twisted fragments of a strange metal object were upon the back, fastened to the white shoulders with metal clamps that gripped them cruelly!

It was evident that something, recently torn away, had been fastened to the back of the girl!

Sam brought a file from the machine. I helped aimlessly, mechanically, and we cut that metal frame off. As we worked over that white body, with its soft tints of green, I saw strange, livid marks upon the back, which stood out sharply from the warm hue of the skin. I had never seen anything like them. They were splotches of a dull violet color. They looked like burns, or stains, that must have been caused by the thing that had been fastened to her body.

"Radium burns?" I questioned Sam in apathetic curiosity.

"No. Something similar, perhaps. Radium emanations whiten the hair, but the color of the skin is not affected except by inflammation. This is the effect of atomic radiation of a shorter wavelength, I think. My hands were oddly stained for months while I was making my initial experiments with the artificial generation of the cosmic ray, which led to the hydrodyne. I found the cause and developed an effective treatment. I imagine that burn is the chief cause of her coma."

"Coma! Then she isn't—" My heart beat madly, and a mist came before my eyes.

"I think there is hope. She seems not to have been injured by the monster, or to have been seriously hurt by the fall. She is in a profoundly comatose state, due to the electronic burns, and also to physical exhaustion and the terrible hardships of which her appearance gives evidence."

"If you can save her—" I fell on my knees and raised that delicate head in my arms.

"Let's get her to the machine. It's cooler in there. We'll do what we can."

I picked up the silent body, still warm and limp, and carried it to the machine, up to the deck, and down into the cabin. I gently placed it on the divan, and nervously urged Sam to haste.

He deliberately began his work. He had included medical supplies in our equipment; and he was a doctor of considerable skill, whose special knowledge of the effects of etheric vibration was of greatest value here. I could do little except stand and watch him, or stride impatiently up and down the room.

First he quickly prepared a thick red liquid, with which he bathed the violet-colored burns. Then, he made a hypodermic injection, and next administered a small quantity of some kind of gas—a mixture of nitrous oxide, or laughing gas, with something else that I did not recognize. In a few minutes the beating of the heart had become normal, and the breathing was resumed. He had me cover the patient up, and it soon became evident that she had passed into a deep but natural sleep.

I sat by the couch, feasting my sight on the reality of the vision that had been mine so long, in a fever of impatience for the time the beautiful sleeper might awake, so that I could speak to her, yet fearful of making a sound that would disturb her.

Sam had gone out to examine the dead monster more fully. In half an hour he came back in the cabin, carrying a queer writhing green thing in his hand. He held it up silently for me too see. With a sickening sensation, I perceived that it was a miniature replica of the great flying monster!

It was no bigger than a dove. The madly fluttering wings were a bright rich green, very delicate and soft. The thin, slender tentacles that clutched Sam's hand, or scratched harmlessly at it with undeveloped claws, were a pale rose color. The thin, fishlike body was almost white, and the little bloom at the end of it was now an intense violet in color, while the little black sense organs were thrust stiffly out of it.

"Quite a find," Sam said. "We ought to learn no end of things from studying it, if we can keep it alive."

"Quiet," I whispered. "Don't wake her. But where did you get it?"

"Tore it out of a curious pouch on the back of the old one. A cunning little creature, isn't it?"

"Not to my way of looking at it."

"I wonder what it eats? Most likely it's carnivorous. The claws would suggest as much. And that assumption would demand that there must be large game of some kind to support the winged plants."

Sam carried the little monster on into the galley. In half an hour—since he had still not come out—I left the sleeping girl and went in to see him, fearing that he had been bitten or stung by the thing. I found him with the grotesque little creature perched contentedly on his finger, sucking with the thin pink tentacles at a wisp of cotton he had soaked in condensed milk. An odd thing I noticed about it. The little bloom on the end of the body, which had been purple a short time before, was now white, flushed only with a pale pink glow.

"It's as friendly as a kitten," Sam said. "I'm going to name it Alexander. No reason why it should not develop into a young conqueror."

"Keep it, and give me a pet rattlesnake!"

And it was well he did keep it.

CHAPTER SIXTEEN
Xenora of Lothar

I WENT back to the beautiful sleeping girl, and sat down again in my rapt contemplation of the quiet charm of her face. She was breathing quite normally, and the face bore a slight smile of pleasure. Suddenly she moved, and the eyelids were raised. Clear violet eyes looked straight into mine—they were those eyes that have haunted me always.

"Melvin Dane?" she breathed in a voice that was low and musical and wholly delicious. She knew me! She spoke my name! Truly, it was the Green Girl! She was aware of the meeting of our minds upon the ether. "My chieftain of dreams."

From beneath the light covers she reached a slender rounded arm, white, with just a hint of green tan. I took her hand in my own, feeling a strange thrill at the touch. After a moment of hesitation, when I struggled fiercely with that thrill, relaxing to it briefly, I put her hand quickly to my lips, and then released it.

I did not feel capable of speech. For all the hours since we had found the girl, I had been undergoing a storm of emotions—alternate joy and despair. Now, when the Green Girl actually smiled upon me, I forgot all my old dreams of how I would cross oceans and voyage through space to take her in my arms. I sat still, with a curious lump in my throat, in incredulous joy, not daring even to surrender to the delicious thrill of her touch.

She laughed softly, and questioned, "From whence did you come, chieftain of my dreams, or am I dreaming still?"

"It's no dream," I began awkwardly. "Though I can hardly feel that it isn't. I came from a land above the red sky. I have always dreamed of you! And now I find you real— living! What is your name? Do you have people?"

"I am Xenora. My father was the last prince of the old city of Lothar. My people now are few."

"You spoke my name. You already knew it?"

"Yes, Melvin Dane, I have dreamed of you since I was a child. Even now, before I awoke, I had a curious dream of you—I thought you were coming to me through the sky in a ship of fire." The poor girl had raised herself on her elbow. Now she lay back on the pillows again as if she were very weak.

"So you have known me always, too?"

"Since one day when I was a child. The old lost city was my playground, and even when I was very small I wandered alone through the great palaces of old Lothar, dreaming of the ancient time when her warriors were great. One day I found a strange machine in a ruined tower room. Curious sounds came out of it when I put it to my ears. And then came the vision of you—of the white prince of my dreams. Day after day I slipped back, to dream of you. But even when I could go back no longer, you still came to me in dreams."

"But now they are dreams no longer. You are mine!" I exulted.

I thought there was something wistful in her smile, a hint of sadness in her sparkling violet eyes. "Yes," she breathed, "even for a little time, it is real. A little time, before the end."

She rose a little, resting on her elbow. I took her hand again. How slender and small it was. She still smiled, a little wanly.

"Don't speak of the end." I said, unconsciously lapsing into the strange tongue in which I had so often conversed with her. "I have found you. You are safe. The flying thing is dead."

For a moment there was frank admiration in her violet eyes that went oddly to my head. "You killed it! You are like the great warriors of old!"

"Hardly," I demurred with painful honesty. "I did nothing except push down a little pin."

"But the Lunak, the flying thing, is not what I fear. It had taken me from a fate that was far worse. It was carrying me from the power of the Lord of Flame!"

Her eyes dilated as she pronounced the words, as if they were a curse of fatal horror. For a moment she seemed to struggle fiercely with some terrible fear. She sank back rigid and unconscious to the couch. I sprang to her and lifted her in my arms. I started to call Sam, but in a moment her body relaxed, and her breathing was resumed, though she did not open her eyes.

Still, I felt no haste to put her down. I brought her a little closer to my heart, and my lips were very close indeed to hers when suddenly her violet eyes opened wide. I almost dropped her in my speechless confusion, and I felt myself turning red. Embarrassed more than I care to say, I hurriedly departed for the galley.

I found Sam whistling cheerfully and busy making apple pies for dinner. I have known several men who called themselves scientists, but Sam is the only one of them who had mastered the science of cooking. He used to say that if he were going to be hanged, he would want to cook and eat his dinner first.

"What did you do with the little—reptile-plant?" I asked.

"Oh, Alexander's gone to bed," he said lightly, pointing to a ventilated cardboard box on the shelves. "But how are you coming on with your specimen?" he questioned with a grin.

"Xenora seems—er—recovering very well. Perhaps you had better see her. She might think—that I—"

As Sam, with an understanding nod, walked toward the cabin door, I climbed out on deck, to think about it all. The great trees still whispered a little in the hot south wind, which was laden with the unfamiliar fragrance of the great purple flowers. The rich green grass moved in long waves before it. The red glare still beat down with a torrid intensity. I gazed up the vast slope of purple and green, to the blue cliffs in the distant north, and wondered about what the girl had told me—and about what she thought of me now. I cursed myself for my impulsive action.

A city of ruined palaces! A fallen race that had had a science great enough to build a radio machine—if such it was—which she had found and over which our minds had met. And a thing more terrible, and the flying plants! What had she meant by the words, "The Lord of Flame," the mere utterance of which had overwhelmed her with horror?

Then I thought again of the metal bands and frame we had cut from her body, and of the strange burns upon her skin. What was it that had caused them? Did all of that link up with the menace that threatened the earth? That might even now be doing its work?

CHAPTER SEVENTEEN
The Lord of Flame

I MUST HAVE STOOD there many minutes, lost in fearful reverie. Unconsciously I heard Sam and Xenora moving about below, heard faintly the murmur of their conversation. At last my grim forebodings of the horror that was to come were interrupted by Sam's cheerful hail, and I went below. I came upon Xenora in the cabin. She was arrayed in a fresh suit of my white flannels that Sam had laid out for her; and evidently she had been under the shower, for drops of water still gleamed on her dark hair. She looked freshly, incredibly beautiful, dressed even as she was.

I must have flushed somewhat, for she laughed at me. But she showed no anger or displeasure—she had not resented what I had done. She looked squarely at me with those cool violet eyes that shone with humor and human feeling. I read honest understanding in their clear depths, and suddenly I went to her and held out my hands. She took them in her slender ones.

Presently we went in together to Sam's wonderful feast. He had the little dining room spick and span as usual, with the windows screened and the white lights going to shut out the terrible red glare. It was very cool in the soft breezes from the fans, and we three sat down in comfort to the delicacies he had prepared.

Sam still remembered what I had taught him, so many years ago, of Xenora's language, so that he was able to converse in it. "It'll be some revelation to the old deadheads at the Academy if we ever get back and publish our account," he said. "They have never admitted telepathy, just because the phenomenon of thought transference depends upon such delicate attunement of minds that it cannot be reproduced at will. Of course, we don't know just how much the radio had to do with it in your case. Undoubtedly it served as a carrying wave, at first at least. But anyhow, it would be some bombshell to toss among my old associates!"

"Who cares what they think about it?" I said. "We've found her. That's all that matters."

Xenora sat down eagerly. I found joy in watching her eat. She manipulated her unfamiliar fork with instinctive culture, and seemed to like Sam's viands immensely. And she ate with the restrained eagerness of one who has not touched food for some time. What misfortunes had the brave girl been through?

Presently, when she was somewhat satisfied, Sam began questioning her in an effort to find out something of the strange world about us. "Where do your people live?" he began.

"Once Lothar was an empire that girdled the central sea. But many lifetimes ago the evil power of Mutron arose, and our people were conquered by the slaves of the Lord of Flame. Now there are but a handful of my race, living in the forests by the northern cliffs. And even they are taken to serve the Lord of Flame—"

"The Lord of Flame. What is that?" Sam asked in amazement.

"It is a dreadful thing—a serpent of green fire that dwells in the violet mists of the chasm of Xath," she said hastily. "But let us not speak of it. No man speaks of the Lord of Flame, for it hears—stay! Oh, horror! Do you not—feel it?"

And indeed, at her words, I felt a strange and alien thrill, as if the revealing searchlight of some dreadful power had been suddenly thrown upon me, as if some strange wind of fear had blown upon my soul. I shivered involuntarily, and crouched closer to the others, trying to drive the horror from my mind.

"God!" Sam breathed hoarsely. "What can we be up against?"

In a moment the girl went hurriedly on, as though to change our thoughts to other things. "Many sleeps ago I was taken by the men of Mutron, and put in the power of Xath. They sent me on a ship to fight the Lunaks. We fell in with a vast number of them, and they brought the vessel down. The fire-crystal was torn from my back in the wreck, and I was free. I ran for the trees, but the Lunaks caught me. And that was the last I knew, until I woke, from my dream of—of—"

She turned to me with a little smile, as if such weirdly incredible adventures were to be taken as a matter of course. I could not speak for the pity and horror that were mingled with my admiration for her courage. But I could, and did, reach under the table and take her hand. Thereafter each of us contrived—after a fashion—to eat with one hand.

That brief and puzzling account of her adventures was all that Xenora was able to give us until experience would enlarge our common vocabularies. Certainly it offered plenty of food for conjecture. She had little scientific knowledge; and when Sam continued his questions, the accounts she gave of the origin and meaning of the strange things she mentioned smacked more of myth than of history.

"Has the Lord of Flame always been, Xenora?"

"No," the Green Girl answered. "Back in the beginning, ten thousand lifetimes past, the men of Lothar ruled, and there was no Mutron to carry them to Xath. The warriors of Lothar were very brave. They fought the Lunaks, and hunted the beasts of the plain. The kings of Lothar reigned in a hundred cities that ringed the central sea, and there was food and joy for all.

"But the Lunaks were very wise. When the great men of Lothar brought weapons of fire to fight them, they went into the jungle and laid an egg, and guarded it, and there sprang up the Lord of Flame! It is a serpent of green fire, as thick as a mountain and as long as a river! All the warriors of Lothar went to meet it, and it slew them with a breath of fire! It took slaves of our people and carried them into the fire-pit of Xath.

"And from that day, through countless lifetimes, our people have been worshipers and slaves of the Lord of Flame. Those who are taken are no longer as men, but as sleepers walking, with the fire-crystal on their backs. They fly in ships of Mutron, the City of the Sleepers, and rule with a heavy hand in the name of the Lord of Flame. None escape them."

"Well, I'll be d—er—flabbergasted!" Sam exploded. His face was a study. Incredulous disbelief was there, and amazement, and something of fear and horror, too. What the girl said had all the earmarks of a fairy tale. But we had seen the metal upon her body, and the purple stains—and we had felt that sudden, inexplicable wave of fear.

"Is it possible? Mel, it can't be! It's too fantastic!"

I could make no answer. "And you, Xenora. You were taken by that thing?" I cried in sudden horror.

"I was taken in a ship, and carried to Mutron, the City of Fear. There they fastened on me the fire-crystal. Then my mind was in a sleep, and my limbs did not what I willed. Until the ship fell my life was a nightmare of toil and terror. The Lunak took me, and I knew nothing until you found me."

Xenora still seemed rather weak and tired from her terrible ordeal. After we had eaten, Sam and I conducted her over the ship, with a view to convincing her of the wonderful power of the machine and thus to quiet her fear of that mysterious menace. We started the engines and moved the machine a little. I fired the gun for her edification, to show how the monster had been killed, and Sam showed her how to blow the siren, and even let her pull the cord. Then we took her back to a stateroom, and turned it over to her.

As she went into the room, Sam proposed that he and I go hunting. His real object, I think, was to get some fresh meat for the little winged plant, but we wished to learn as much as possible of the fauna and flora about us.

I was not eager to leave the machine, but we were armed with the best of weapons, and there seemed to be little danger. Then, we intended to be gone only a few minutes. When we were ready to start I tapped on Xenora's door, to tell her that we were leaving, but she made no answer. I supposed that she was already asleep.

We climbed up on deck, and closed the hatch behind us.

CHAPTER EIGHTEEN
Lost in the Purple Forest

WE WALKED off east through the level green meadows, beneath the scattered trees that were bright with purple bloom. For my own part, I was much more interested in the vegetation than in any game we might come upon. In fact, I would not have been greatly disappointed if our hunt had been in vain.

The leaves of what I have called grass were really so wide and thick that it was hardly grass at all. The higher stems of it bore myriads of tiny, bright-red flowers. The great trees were, in shape and foliage, somewhat like the oak, though the rich profusion of the purple flowers almost concealed the leaves. They bore small fruits, in appearance a little like the date, which, as we were later to learn, were edible. But, in all the time I was in that strange world, I found no single plant that was exactly like any I had known above.

Indeed that was a strange hunt, under a flaming scarlet sky, nine miles beneath the ocean, through forests of the purple trees that burdened the air with their unfamiliar fragrance, in search of we knew not what in the way of game.

We tramped steadily eastward over the green meadows for perhaps half an hour, rewarded with the sight of no living thing. The Omnimobile had long been out of sight. We crossed a low grassy ridge and made our way out across another broad smooth valley.

At last, as we looked from a screen of brush at the edge of a little meadow, we saw an odd-looking creature gazing unalarmed a hundred yards away. It was somewhat larger than a hog, with gray, hairless skin and long white tusks or horns. It had an oddly heavy, barrel-like body.

It must have smelled us, for it threw up its head with a peculiar squeal, tossing its great tusks. Sam and I both fired. We have never agreed which of us hit it, but it slumped over on the green vegetation. We hurried up to it. It was quite dead. It had great claws, and somewhat resembled a sloth, although it was exactly like nothing that I had ever seen.

Sam took out his knife and skillfully removed half of the skin, wrapping up a piece of meat in it. The beast had thick rolls of fat along the back, but the flesh beneath looked so nice and tender that he took some of it to try for steak.

"We'll try some of it broiled when we get back," he anticipated, smacking his lips.

"Let's hurry on," I said. "We've been gone longer than I intended, already. What if Xenora wakes up and we're not there?"

"Let's see," Sam said doubtfully. "The wind was from the south, wasn't it?"

I looked around in sudden panic. I was almost sure that I knew the way back to the machine—almost!

The strange world about us was suddenly very alien and cruel. The plains were lonely and flat and dead. The trees were suddenly wild and mysterious, as if they concealed strange monsters. There was a ghastly, unearthly menace in the red gleam of the sky.

In all directions the country looked much the same. There was no definite landmark. We stood there for a time, scanning the unfamiliar panorama, in the beginning of panic. There were half a dozen groups of trees, any of which might have been the one from which we fired. It occurred to me that it would be very inconvenient if one of the flying plants came along, and I began to think of other things that might happen. I came to a tardy realization of our helplessness and utter ignorance of the dangers that might surround us.

The purple trees and the scarlet sky seemed to leer at us, to gather closer, to laugh in fiendish joy at the unnamable doom they might have in store for us. Unconsciously I drew my pistol, and my muscles were involuntarily tensed, so that I started when Sam spoke.

"Of course we can see the wall of cliffs in the north. That will give us the general direction. If we can get up on that hill, we might be able to see the machine."

He pointed toward a round, bare, green hilltop that rose several hundred feet toward the red sky. It was perhaps a mile away, in the direction of the hazy blue cliffs. He slung the piece of meat over his shoulder and we set out over the open field. It was very hot, and the perspiration was dripping from us. I had hardly noticed the damp, hot wind before, but now it felt like a blast from a furnace. The intense scarlet radiation of the flaming sky dried up our energy. The steady beam of heat brought over us a growing languor, a depressed and spiritless weariness.

The whole weird region was very still. The only sounds were the soft sighing of the wind in the trees, and the thrashing and rustling of our feet in the rank grass. The tiny scarlet flowers danced before the wind almost like little insects, and a few brilliant petals blew sometimes from one of the sparsely scattered trees.

"Phew!" Sam whistled, stopping to mop his brow with the huge red bandanna he had tied around his neck. "This is beginning to feel like the Sahara. I'm glad I didn't happen to be a native of the place. You bet the machine will look good, when we find it!"

"If we find it," I could not refrain from saying.

In five minutes more we were far up the side of the little hill. The side of the eminence was bare of the great flowering trees, so the strange forest lay about us southward for many miles. Eagerly we looked in the direction that should have been southwest, for the Omnimobile.

A vast stretch of the rolling plateau lay before our eyes, low verdant hills, and vast green meadows, scattered with the brilliant purple trees, singly and in groves. Far away, all across the southern horizon, stretched the black sea on which we had landed, glancing with the crimson light of the sky. But nowhere, in all that vast strange expanse, did we catch a glimpse of the machine.

"It must be just in a low place," Sam said hopefully. "Or, I think I remember now that there was a little grove just north of it. We will see it in a minute, if we climb higher up."

"I hope so," I said, raising my binoculars for a better look.

"And we have compasses and instruments to guide ourselves around the world, if we'd just thought to bring them!"

"It's no use," I said. "Let's go on to the top."

CHAPTER NINETEEN
The Hill of Horror

WE CLIMBED UP the last few yards to the summit, and gazed across toward the dim blue cliffs that rimmed this world on the north. We stood on a great divide. A vast valley lay before us, stretching away until it was veiled with a faint rosy haze. The curious checkered expanse of green plain and purple woodland sloped far, far away to the north. Perhaps twenty miles away was the vague outline of a great silver lake, dyed with the light of the crimson sky.

Just back of the lake seemed to be a shore of low black cliffs. And beyond those ragged peaks, and beneath the towering and rugged columns of blue that threw themselves up to the bloody sky, was a strange sight indeed!

There was a weird flicker of dancing lights in that far-flung crimson mist, as if it reflected strange infernal fires in a pit behind the low black wall. There were faint and moving gleams of violet—of pale violet flames that changed and rose and fell. Vague tongues of violet fire wove themselves throughout that distant rose-colored mist, with a writhing, rhythmic motion. They formed curious shapes of flame that faded strangely and came again!

But my description is futile. The important thing was not what we saw, but what we *felt!* A curiously unpleasant sensation of helplessness, and of strange horror, came over me. I felt as if I were stealing a forbidden glimpse of an ancient and incredible hell! Fear swept over me—alien, inconceivable terror—like a keen and bitter wind that numbed my brain! I felt the horror of a sentient force, utterly inhuman, devoid of all human knowledge or understanding, as cold and remote as the frozen night of space!

It was terrible—an intangible aura of fear that reached out of that pit and tugged at our souls with the icy hand of stark horror. I can give the world no conception of the overwhelming terror of it! Nor would I if I could, for such things are better forgotten. I dropped my rifle and clenched my hands, trembling. I braced my feet as though against the force of a physical wind that was striving to carry me toward that abyss of nebulous horror-light!

I looked at Sam. He stood very still, leaning back, with hands raised and jaw dropped. In his eyes was the look of the fresh and innocent soul that struggles with a pitiless terror that it cannot know or understand. Such a look I had never seen before—and God grant that I may never see it again.

My gaze was drawn irresistibly back into that mantle of moving light. Even as I watched, a pillar of green flame, very bright and broad, thrust itself up through the wavering mist of violet fire, and into the crimson haze. It was like the slender head of some obscene green reptile. It reached up— incredibly. It writhed and twisted about! It *was* like a great serpent of fire. And it *saw* us!

It grew still with awful attention. Eternities seemed to pass as the dreadful thing hung there, motionless, like a vast frozen pillar of twisted emerald flame, like a column of curdled green fire, with curious throbbing changes in its brightness. I felt a weird force flowing out of it. And I knew that it was *watching us!*

"My God!" Sam muttered. "My God!" I looked at him again. His thin face was very white, and beaded with perspiration. He was mechanically mopping at his forehead with the red handkerchief, and staring at the mist of flame with the glaze of terror upon his eyes.

I struggled mightily to throw off the spell of amazement and terror—of alien and unutterable horror—that was grasping at my mind. It was a heart-breaking effort. I moved. I seized Sam's arm and shook it. He swayed drunkenly, with his eyes still on the awful lights. He was like one in a trance—like a man in a dream of death!

And I felt those icy fingers of unthinkable doom closing about my own mind. I was paralyzed again, with my eyes drawn back to the north. The snake's head of frozen green still throbbed strangely, and the flickering violet aurora still kept up its storm of varying motion, in the dim rosy haze into which the awful head was lifted.

Something was reaching toward us, out of the pit! I knew there was intelligence in it—a *will*, inhuman, and unthinkably strong! It was calling us, compelling us! I knew that in a few moments we could fight no more.

Suddenly a low sobbing sound reached us on that warm, humid south wind, a sound that wailed uncertainly behind us, and rose to a piercing shriek, and slowly died away into the distant south, echoing weirdly on hills and trees as it rolled and sank.

Sam started with a hoarse cry, and went off down the hill toward the north at a stumbling run—toward that abyss of alien horror! A moment more I struggled desperately, but that pitiless power overwhelmed me! I followed in his tracks!

And then, a clear rich voice reached me from beyond the hill—a shout in Xenora's rich and ringing tones. It had a clear human overtone of confidence and courage. "Come back, Melvin Dane! Come back, Sam!"

The old scientist stopped uncertainly, passing his hand dazedly before his brow. Abruptly the terror was gone from my mind. The love and the courage of the brave girl flowed into me. And suddenly, with the green light still pulsing through it, as though sent by a mighty heart, the terrible thing in the north dimmed slowly and faded away! Still the violet lances flickered through the rosy mist, but the green thing was gone—and we were free!

I took Sam's hand, and we turned our backs on the amazing play of fire above the incredible pit, and hastened to the trees from which Xenora's voice had seemed to come. We reached the little grove, but I did not see the girl. Suddenly I had the persuasion that I had not actually heard her with my ears, after all!

"Xenora! Xenora! Are you here?" I called uncertainly.

Sam was still trembling and mopping at his forehead. "She wasn't really here, I think, Mel," he presently said in a strained voice. "She must have reached us with telepathy."

For a long time then we stood there under the flowering trees—very close together, feeling all the awful mystery of the strange world about us—and thinking of what had happened.

"What was it?" My silent lips at last formed the question.

" 'The Lord of Flame!' Xenora said. 'The Lord of Flame!' 'A serpent of green fire that dwells in Xath below Mutron!' Sam repeated mechanically. "I would to God I knew what it is!"

"And what was that awful sound?"

"That was the siren of the Omnimobile, I think. You know we showed Xenora how to operate it. Probably that saved us, by attracting our minds from the Thing while Xenora reached us."

"Then if we go toward it—"

At that instant the wild, sobbing shriek rose again, very welcome for all the wailing qualities of its tones. In a moment we were hastening down the green hillside among the purple trees, in the direction from which the sound had come. Twice we heard it again. And in half an hour we saw the glint of the silver metal side of the machine beyond a thicket of purple bloom.

I have seen few more welcome sights than the Omnimobile was then. The heaviness of it, the threatening nose of the little gun, the air of irresistible power about it, and even its clumsy, beast-like appearance were reassuring. Sam gave a cheer, and we made the last hundred yards at a run. At last we stumbled up the metal ladder and stood upon the narrow deck again.

We clambered through the manhole. The white electric light of the interior was in strange contrast to the crimson gloom, and the coolness of the air was very refreshing. Xenora was in the cabin, anxiously on her feet.

"It was the Lord of Flame," she whispered. "And you escaped."

"Thanks to you, my dream girl," I said, taking her boldly in my arms.

CHAPTER TWENTY
Sam's Pet

"I FELT IT WATCHING you—calling you—and I pulled the cord that makes the great cry," Xenora whispered, after a long, long time.

"Thank God you did. It saved us. We were lost!" And I told her of the amazing storm of flames, of the Thing that had risen out of them, and of the irresistible spell of terror, from which she had awakened us.

"Yes," she said. "It was the Lord of Flame. He watches the world from Xath. He knows the acts of every man."

I must have reeled a little with fatigue, for suddenly the girl looked at me with quick sympathy brimming in her eyes. "But you—my white prince of dreams—you are very tired. You must rest."

Abruptly I realized that I was tired, dead with fatigue, with an unutterable weariness not only of body but of mind, for the horror had exhausted my emotions. I heard Sam splashing water under the shower. I followed him to the bathroom, and then went to my bunk in the stern, for I had given Xenora my stateroom. I was leaden with weariness, but peacefully secure in the protection of the heavy metal walls of the Omnimobile.

I have very little idea how long I slept, for we had let our watches run down. In the absence of the sun, we came to pay less and less attention to the time, though we usually kept the chronometers going.

When I woke I felt greatly refreshed, with my terrorized despair almost gone. But I would not forget the sense of evil and intelligent power that I had got from the pillar of strange green fire that had been thrust so deliberately and purposefully up through the mist of violet flame, and into the rosy haze that hung over the hidden abyss in which it lurked.

It had *seen* us! I knew it. And I knew that, even if its incredible power seemed withdrawn, it was still not far away.

I heard Sam speak, heard Xenora laugh. Evidently they were in the little galley, for I heard the clatter of cooking utensils. I dressed and went in. How beautiful the girl was! Her red lips were brilliant against the light green tan of her skin. Her dark hair fell over her shoulders in a rich cascade, and her violet eyes were sparkling with life.

She came to me quickly and took my hand. No words passed between us, for our minds were too near together to need many words. It was enough for me to see the sympathy and love in her eyes. And it seemed again, when our hands met, that a subtle current flowed back and forth between us, setting our minds alight, making our hearts beat faster, raising us together into a higher ethereal plane and fusing our beings into one.

In a moment Sam, with a kind smile of understanding on his face, called us to the table. The steak from the thing we had killed was a great success, and the table was loaded with the good things with which the larder of the machine was stocked. The girl ate heartily, as did Sam and I, and we talked and laughed a good deal. Even if the small number of our common experiences limited the topics of conversation, we had a merry enough time of it, and somehow that happy meal gave us greater courage to meet the strange menace that rose before us.

After we had eaten, and all had helped wash the dishes, all in the same gay spirit, Sam got out the box in which he had put the little creature he had named Alexander. I had quite forgotten all about the diminutive winged plant. With mingled curiosity and repulsion I watched him unfasten the box. I had not yet recovered from my instinctive horror at sight of the flying plants. Xenora seemed to share my antipathy toward them. But Sam has always seemed to care as much for wild life as for men; and he seemed to consider the little creature as natural a pet as a dog. However, of course, his real reason for keeping it was for scientific observation.

The thing fluttered about in the box when he picked it up, and as soon as the lid was raised, it flew out and lit on his hand. Already it seemed bigger and stronger than it had been a day before. The pale yellow of the little fish-like body was darkening. The wings seemed a darker green, and stronger. The blood-color of the slender tentacles along the sides of the body was growing deeper and deeper.

The weird little monster clung to his finger with three of its tentacles, holding the thin, petal-like membranes about its head extended, and moving its black, knobbed organs restlessly. At first the color of the flower-like tissues was almost white, but when I made a sudden motion, they quickly darkened to a deep violet, and the little creature crouched down in Sam's hand as if it were alarmed.

Sam smiled down at it with real understanding in his face. He uncovered on the table a dish containing a great chunk of the raw, bloody meat of the thing we had killed. The queer, flower-like head twisted about, and the black, stalked organs moved like eyes. Abruptly the membrane changed color again, from the violet of its fright to a deep red.

Sam held his hand over the meat and the slender tentacles disengaged themselves and writhed down over the plate like tiny red snakes. They began to suck the juices out of the meat, and—as the thing filled itself—the strange flower slowly faded in color, until it was a pale pink.

Observing my instinctive horror of the thing, Sam said: "That's the way it was meant to eat, Mel. Nothing unnatural about it. Our table manners might not seem very elegant to an angel!"

"I guess you're right. But that thing just gets on my nerves." When he went to put the little creature back in the box, it clung to his finger as if reluctant to go, and strange bright patterns of color flashed over the thin membrane. It seemed fantastic enough, but even then I was sure that the little thing possessed intelligence, and that it was beginning to feel affection for Sam.

The next time he took it out it seemed larger and stronger and hungrier! We stayed there for what must have been ten days, though we kept no accurate account of time. It grew rather astonishingly, and always its odd appearance of intelligence was greater. It seemed to feel a real affection for Sam. He whistled ancient tunes to it sometimes, and it seemed to listen in great delight. And for long hours he would sit with the thing in his lap and talk to it. He declared that it was getting so that it could understand. Bright colors crawled on the membranous fringe, and it seemed to listen to him with great intentness.

CHAPTER TWENTY-ONE
Back to the Haunted Hill

ON THE MORNING—if one may speak of morning in that world of eternal day—after we had slept off the fatigue of our visit to the hill where we had seen the lights of terror, Sam took me aside for a short talk.

"Mel," he said, "we can't forget what we've come here for. My generator is still keeping up the interference in the ether; but sooner or later the force we have come to fight—and it must be that 'Lord of Flame' of Xenora's, and the thing we saw from the hill—will break down the interference. And then the Earth—will freeze!"

"But what can we do against—that? And Xenora! Sam, I can't leave her. She's worth more to me than the Earth. There's plenty of room in here for us to live our lives out. I've been thinking about it—and I can't go."

He nodded sympathetically. "I know, Mel. She means a lot to you. But perhaps we will win and save our lives, too."

"Not a chance," I said bitterly. "Not against that thing we saw. It means death—or worse! But I suppose we have to go on and do our best."

The old man was beaming. He patted me on the shoulder. "I knew you would be with me, when you had time to think," he said. "Now, when the life of the world is at issue, we can't consider ourselves."

"What do you think we can do?"

"What can't we do? We have the Omnimobile. We have machines and tools. We have knowledge, and our hands. We can go anywhere, and do anything! But the first thing is to engage in study, to find out what we have to deal with, and how to fight it."

"I suppose so."

"Mel, we must go back to that hill."

"No! Not there! It was only a miracle—and Xenora—- that saved us before!"

"I've some theories. We'll be better prepared next time."

A sudden thought struck me. "Say, couldn't we pay a flying visit to our own world again, and tell what we've found? Then the world would still have a chance, when we are—gone. A half-million Americans, with tanks and heavy artillery, would look mighty good down here. And it would just take a day or two to go."

"No," Sam said. "The world would hardly believe it all, even if we carried out what evidence we could. And nothing could be done in time. Then, I'm not sure we could get out. In fact, I'm pretty sure we couldn't. The rockets might carry us three miles high, all right; but we could never break through that water from beneath. We would fall back. Mel, it's up to us…"

During the days that followed, Sam spent most of his hours in the little laboratory. He spent much time on those great machines that controlled his forces in the ether. And he invented and developed another device that was more nearly within my understanding.

"You know, Mel," he said one day, "I think I can rig up something to protect us from that—fear—that came so near getting us. Ever since you made your telepathic contact with the Green Girl, I have had the idea that the brain sets up disturbances in the ether. We know that the action of the nervous system is electrical in nature, and all electric discharges set up ether waves. It happened that you and she had great minds, created in perfect synchronism, so that each was sensitive to the vibrations of the other. Hypnotism is best explained by such electric theories.

"Now, I am convinced that the 'Lord of Flame' is a brain—whether in a human body or not I cannot attempt to say. It creates such powerful etheric disturbances that it was able to affect us at a distance. If that is the case, it ought to be a fairly simple matter to provide insulation against its vibrations. You know that induction or electric action cannot penetrate a conducting cage. I ought to be able to fix a conducting helmet that will prevent the induction of neuronic currents in our brains."

A short time after, he showed me three helmets, as he called them. They were little more than bags of wire gauze to be put over our heads. He demonstrated that an electroscope draped with one of them remained entirely unaffected by charges brought near it; but it seemed a ridiculously inadequate protection against that terror.

We went hunting several times, for the benefit of the little plant. After the first few days, Sam let it go along, hanging on his coat. It was growing very fast, and developing remarkable characteristics. It showed surprising intelligence. Sam seemed to have a real affection for it, and it, in turn, seemed to love him.

I never ceased to feel the strangeness of those expeditions over the rolling green grasslands, among the sparsely scattered flowering trees, in the hot damp air and the intense red light. We shot two more animals like the first, and three others of a smaller variety, which somewhat resembled large rabbits.

Very shortly after Sam had perfected his electro-screen helmets, he planned another expedition to the hill where we had so nearly met incredible disaster. We carried a telescope, electrometers, spectroscope, and a few pieces of Sam's recently developed and highly complicated apparatus, which he had neglected to name, for detecting and analyzing etheric waves.

Xenora insisted on going with us, and there seemed no reason for leaving her behind, since Sam had perfect confidence in the efficacy of his new helmets, and since the girl herself was an excellent woodsman, and could undertake to keep us from getting lost.

We had a long hot march of it across the green plateau among the purple trees, with the fierce beams of the crimson sky pouring down upon us. Burdened with the heavy instruments, we were worn out when we reached the summit. I had suggested that we come in the machine, but Sam wanted to keep it out of the sight of the weird enemy we fought.

Once more we gazed across the vast valley of purple and green, to the mists of ruby light over that abyss beyond the distant lake, in which the violet beams still danced and pulsed. And hardly did we have our apparatus set up when we saw that unearthly, serpent-like beam of green fire writhe up out of the vale of mystery into the rosy haze!

We had on the insulating shields, and I felt nothing of the inexplicable horror of the former occasion; though, of course, the whole adventure was certainly terrible enough. But now that strange thing of green seemed distant and devoid of menace. By way of experiment, I ventured to raise my helmet. The terror caught me like a cold and rushing torrent that swept me almost off my feet! I was glad enough to get the wire gauze fastened back about my head again.

"It is the Lord of Flame," Xenora cried, "looking over toward the city of my people, to see who will be taken to become his slaves. This is a wonderful thing, Barsoni Sam, that lets us not feel its power!"—Barsoni being a word that means "great man," in the tongue of Lothar.

For many minutes the amazing shape of twisting green radiance hung in the air. Sam was busy with his apparatus, squinting at the thing through telescope and spectroscope, and reading his other devices. At last the awful, throbbing thing faded away, and died into nothingness. Only the violet lances were left in the mist.

"Many of my theories were substantiated," Sam informed me, almost jubilant. "And I got a lot of new data. It is rather odd, but the light from that thing shows the helium lines as luminous bands, not as the dark lines that might be expected to rise from the absorption of the helium in this atmosphere. I can hardly understand it."

He said nothing more, but was sunk deep in thought as we quickly gathered the instruments and hastened silently down the hill. I felt that he had won a notable victory in the invention of the thought-insulating helmets. We arrived at the machine again without incident.

CHAPTER TWENTY-TWO
The Silver Sphere

FOR SEVERAL DAYS longer, Sam continued his labors in the laboratory. During that time "Alexander," the flying plant, developed remarkably. Before we moved, it had a wingspread of two or three feet. I have spoken of its intelligence. It soon learned to flutter to the guns when we were preparing to hunt. Sam talked to it incessantly, and declared that it could understand him. He said it could even make its thoughts known by the varying pattern of colors on its fringe of brilliant membrane. Presently he had it trained to dry dishes and to do other similar tasks in the galley.

Of course the thing never learned to speak. In fact, it was devoid of vocal organs, and incapable of making a sound, though its hearing seemed to be good enough. It appeared to communicate its emotions and thoughts by means of changes of color in the tissue-like membrane that I have termed a flower. And, from a strictly scientific point of view, communication by light, or sight, is quite as logical as communication by sound.

Sam examined the black, rod-like organs projecting from the flower on the thing, and said that each of them bore thousands of tiny eyes, like the compound eyes of an insect.

After we had been in the vicinity for perhaps two weeks by upper world time, we started the Omnimobile's great motors again, and moved northward. I had not told Xenora about my talk with Sam—our minds were too closely attuned to require much conversation. I knew that she understood that our maneuver would probably mean our sacrifice to the cause of the world. She said nothing of it, but I thought I detected a sadness in her manner.

During all the hours that Sam had been in his laboratory, alone or with Alexander, I had spent most of the time with Xenora. We wandered together about the meadows, or sat in the cabin to escape the almost intolerable heat. Always I loved her more, brimming as she was with humor and sympathy and love. And bitterly I cursed the fate that was dragging us both to our doom!

Even at the beginning, Sam's scientific achievements had been so far above my understanding that I would scarcely comprehend them, and his later speculations regarding the menace of the abyss were so abstruse that I quite failed to follow them. His little workshop forward was crammed with strange machinery, some of it humming incessantly. Indeed, his apparatus was still keeping up the interference that prevented the freezing of the Earth!

Sam had been signally unsuccessful in getting any scientific information from Xenora, for the simple reason that she had none to impart. But, from her geographical knowledge, he attempted to draw a map, showing the locations of Lothar, of Mutron, and of the pit of the Lord of Flame.

It seemed that there was a strip a score of miles in width between the farther blue walls of the abyss and the great lake we had seen. The pit of Xath seemed to be a great crater lying in that strip. On the brink of the crater Xenora located her "City of the Sleepers," or Mutron. The domain of the last city of Lothar, where she had spent her childhood, lay along the cliffs far to the west of there.

Our boldest plan of action would have been to hurl the machine, by means of the rocket tubes, into the abyss in a direct attack on the Lord of Flame; but Sam, for reasons he did not divulge, doubted the success of such a maneuver. He wished to keep up his researches, and possibly to visit the city of Lothar. His apparatus told him that hidden forces were again stirring in the ether.

For ten hours we moved toward the north, making a long detour to westward to keep within a valley, and always trying to take advantage of such cover as was offered by the purple trees. The country was, for the most part, rolling and green, with the great flowering trees dotting the hills and plains but sparsely. The blazing radiation of the eternal crimson day was undiminished, but the temperature fell slightly with increased altitude.

Xenora and I were together at the cabin control-board, driving the machine; and Sam was in the conning tower, with the little gun, ready for emergencies. When we had been moving for some ten hours, we mounted a low, bare hill, and saw in the little green valley before us a thicker forest of the bright purple trees, offering good cover for the machine.

We had crossed the summit, and I had increased the speed to ten miles per hour in haste to reach the trees, in spite of Sam's fear that the operation of the motors at anything like full capacity would create a disturbance in the ether that our hidden enemies would pick up.

Suddenly I saw a strange thing skimming along over the bright forest before us—in our direction! It looked like a bright silver globe, many feet in diameter! It floated a few hundred feet above the trees, drifting smoothly along like a bright metal balloon in a very swift wind. There was no visible propulsive mechanism.

I shouted a warning to Sam through the speaking tube, to stand by his little gun.

Xenora laid a light hand on my shoulder and said, in a tense voice: "It is the Sleepers of Mutron, the slaves of the Lord of Flame. They will fight to death—they know not fear!"

As the silver sphere drifted swiftly and silently down upon us, as though borne by an invisible wind, twice I caught a glimpse of a slender ray of purple flame, which darted out of it and moved searchingly over the bare greensward below. And then a rich purple beam fell suddenly and intensely upon the Omnimobile!

When that misty finger of purple light discovered us, I saw a strange vortex of pale green fire spring up about the globe and reach out in our direction. Suddenly I realized that this ship was of the same appearance as the weird thing that had destroyed our cottage! Small hope, I thought, if that force of atomic disintegration were to be released again!

I heard the rapid crashing of the machine gun, as Sam began to fire, and presently bursts of smoke appeared about the gleaming sphere. But to hit a relatively small and rapidly moving target even a mile away is no mean feat of marksmanship. I drove rapidly for the purple wood, but with little hope of getting there before the terrible red disintegration had melted us away.

Suddenly I heard the drone of some of Sam's new machinery going into action. He had mounted his switches and dials in the conning tower, so he could control it from where he stood. Vivid blue electric flame quivered and flashed over the metal parts of the machine as his new weapons went into play!

The floating globe of silver drifted nearer, and the misty vortex of green fire about us grew more intense. A strange red glow stole over the vegetation around us, and a solitary purple tree ahead burst into crimson flame. Then the sparkling fingers of purple fire reached out at us again from the sphere. I wondered vaguely why the strange force was not acting upon us. I did not know, until it was all over, that Sam's vacuum tubes had set up a repulsive screen in the ether, protecting us from the electronic vortex!

Abruptly an intensely bright, blinding tongue of white flame leapt toward the silver thing from the great platinum electrode on the nose of the Omnimobile! Sam had turned loose his electric arc! The flame struck the globe, impinging upon it like a jet of fire, converting it into a ball of supernal light.

Then it fell!

It plunged toward the forest in a gleaming curve. The green vortex of the disintegrator ray was gone, and the purple fingers shone no longer. The incandescent shell crashed out of sight beyond the purple trees!

CHAPTER TWENTY-THREE
The Green Slaves

SAM SNAPPED OFF the arc as the silver ship fell, and the drumming of the generators stopped. For a little time the world was very still. Xenora stood tense and silent beside me. As I turned toward her, I caught the slight perfume of her dark hair.

Indeed, the Green Girl was a beautiful being! The white flannels she wore failed to conceal the delectable curves of her slight and boyish figure. Her rich, red lips were parted slightly, in the unconscious intensity of her outward gaze.

Abruptly she became conscious of my look, and turned to face me, with a quick smile on her face. There was a radiant, joyous light in her eyes. The soft green tint of her skin was obscured by the rich, warm flush of her excitement, and she smiled with gladness.

Impulsively she reached her slender hand out to take mine. "You have won, Melvin Dane," her soft voice said. "The ship of Mutron is fallen. We shall not be slaves of the Lord of Flame. We shall not die the violet death in the pit of Xath!"

"I hope not, my Xenora," I said. "I hope—" and I stopped in a little confusion. I was not really embarrassed, but I could not go on. Really, talking to a princess like Xenora is quite a different thing from making protestations of love to a being of one's dreams.

"What is it that you hope?" she said quickly, with an impish smile.

Sam saved me by coming in from the turret, begrimed with the smoke of the little cannon. He was a wonderful man. He was still strong, erect, and confident, despite the load of toil and hardship our adventure was putting upon his seventy years. His white hair was tousled, and he was cheerfully loading up his ancient pipe, as calmly as if he were in his own kitchen in Florida.

"Looks like the arc did for 'em all right," he said briskly. "Suppose we get over and take a look. We might pick up something new."

"Very well," I assented, and turned to start the motors. I could not resist a grin at Xenora, who was still regarding me with a speculative smile. She laughed back at me; then was suddenly serious.

"Be careful! The Sleepers of Mutron. They might be alive in the wreck. As long as they breathe, the Lord of Flame rules them!"

I started the generators, and the Omnimobile rolled heavily down across the green slope, and through the fringe of flaming purple trees. In a few minutes we came upon the wreck of the silver car, a great tangle of twisted wreckage, half fused by the electricity, and bent and torn by the fall. It lay in the little open space, with a great tree splintered and smoking under it, and the ground about empurpled with fallen petals. The twisted metal plates gleamed brightly in the light of the scarlet sky.

I stopped the Omnimobile, and we got out and approached the wrecked machine. There was a vast mass of the debris. The globe must have been forty feet in diameter. We spent several minutes in gazing at it from different angles, and then Sam and I climbed into the tangle of bent white plates and massive twisted girders.

The machinery had been too completely destroyed for us to be sure just how it worked. But Sam thought that the shell had carried tanks of water, the gravity of which had been negatived by the emanations from tanks of the same luminous gas that supported the roof of waters, lifting the ship. From the nature of the fragments of electrical machinery we observed, it seemed that the horizontal propulsion was attained by the ionization and repulsion of the helium atoms in the air. The apparatus that had produced the atomic disintegration was too badly wrecked to be identified.

Presently I came upon the body of a man, caught between two twisted bars, and cut half in two. The body was naked. It had a greenish cast that was darker by far than that of Xenora's fair skin. The physique, and the size and shape of the head, showed a race of high intellectual development.

The dead man had a metal frame clamped upon his back. It was twisted and broken, and whatever had been fastened upon his body had been torn away in the crash. And the corpse had upon its back the strange violet stains that had been upon Xenora when we found her!

Presently Sam found another body. It had been half burned up by the arc. It, too, had the metal frame upon it, and the thing the frame was to hold was still clamped to it! The body bore, fastened to the back with those cruel metal clamps, a six-sided bar of blue metal. It was six inches in diameter and two feet long.

"This must be the thing Xenora calls a 'fire crystal,' " Sam said, "though I don't see any fire about it. It's damned queer…"

"Do you suppose there is machinery in the bar, that generates forces or currents that move the man about like a puppet?"

"Might be. I don't know. The metal thing may be a receiver for the occult force set up in the ether by the Lord of Flame—hypnotism by radio, perhaps, or something of the kind."

"Anyhow, as you said, it's damned queer, like everything else we've found here—excepting Xenora."

"Suppose we take the thing along, and open it up when we have time?"

He produced a pair of pliers, and we twisted the odd blue bar out of its frame, and carried it to the machine. It was oddly light to be metal, though it must have been an irksome burden to the one on which it was fastened. We got aboard again, and moved for the cover of the purple wood, for we did not know how soon relief would come for the fallen ship. But Xenora assured us that the Lunaks, as she called the flying things, quite frequently destroyed the ships of Mutron, and that the fate of this one would be laid to them.

CHAPTER TWENTY-FOUR
The Blue Prism

FOR PERHAPS thirty miles we drove the great machine through the brilliant forest, southward down a broad valley. At last we stopped in a little grove of tall flowering trees, close by the cool crystal stream. Beyond the grove was a little patch of green clearing with the great purple trees closing in all about it. It was a peaceful spot, weirdly beautiful, and it seemed secure enough. The unceasing wind was not so hot beneath the great trees, and they shielded us from the burning, crimson glare of the sky.

The Omnimobile seemed safely hidden beneath the masses of purple bloom; and whenever we were tired, or thought ourselves in danger, we could retire to the quiet security of its cool interior, behind the thick metal walls. Frankly, I hoped that our stay there would be a long one. I tried to forget the menace that hung over the Earth.

Our life there was simple, and for my part, I was supremely happy. Or not quite supremely, for I could not quite still my conscience. I was pretty well resigned to fate, however. With such a girl as Xenora, a man might be supremely happy anywhere. We tramped together about the grove, gathered the tiny, bright-red flowers in the green meadows, and bathed in the cool dark pools, where the river flowed beneath the purple trees. Sometimes she sang to me the folk songs of her people, monuments of the high estate that Lothar had once enjoyed.

What would it matter to me if the eternal death came again and forever to the upper Earth? What would it matter if the Earth did freeze? I forgot in the idyllic happiness of Xenora's companionship—or tried to forget. If the roof of water were changed to ice it would only be more secure! The maiden and I could live out our lives in this strange land, without regard to the fate of the world. One of her matchless smiles, or a note of her golden laughter, was worth more than all the Earth!

Meanwhile, Sam was immersed in his laboratory work, in the examination of the prism of blue metal, and in his curious pet. The plant creature still grew with remarkable speed, and always showed most remarkable intelligence. It was always with Sam, flapping along above him on broad green wings, or walking awkwardly upon its thickening red tentacles. Sam gazed at the flickering colors of the membranes about the head, with the light of strange understanding in his eyes, making strange gestures with his hands. Just to what extent they could communicate, I never knew.

It always went with him, when he went to hunt for its meat. It was a voracious eater, requiring a kill a day. The great sloth-like animals were plentiful and sluggish; it was not difficult to stalk them. As soon as it was strong enough, the plant creature learned to carry Sam's rifle. Its extraordinary intelligence, or imitative instinct, is shown by the fact that one day it fired the gun itself, when it was flying with the weapon, and saw one of the sloths on the run.

It showed a very real affection for Sam. Once, when they were out together, it saved his life. One of the tuskers had suddenly charged him from behind, and the creature flew at it and attacked it madly with its undeveloped claws. At the cost of considerable minor injury to itself, it held the beast off until Sam could get in a shot. It always showed an odd delight at his caresses, and seemed to take a peculiar joy in the music of his old phonograph.

As I have said, it grew very quickly. At the time we stopped in the wood, it was somewhat smaller than a hawk. Perhaps two months later (time was rather meaningless to us during that one happy period of our adventures in that world of unending day) the creature had grown so large that once, in an apparently playful mood, it was able to lift Sam and fly with him on a circuit of a hundred yards, bringing him back to the machine and setting him down very softly. Then its armored brown body was as large as a man, and the green wings were like sails.

That was near the end.

During all that period, Sam devoted much time to the examination of that bar of strangely lit, bright blue metal. He felt that in it he might find a solution to the mystery of the Lord of Flame. I assisted him as much as I could. The metal was evidently an alloy. Analysis showed that it consisted largely of aluminum. There was a trace of a heavy metal that we could not identify. And the bar was slightly, very slightly, radioactive—perhaps, Sam thought, merely because it had been exposed to intense radium emanations.

The density of the bar was only half that of aluminum. For some time we could not understand that. Careful examination showed no break in the surface; and presently we sawed it in two, and then in many pieces, searching for the machinery that we half-expected to find. But, as far as we could determine, the bar was absolutely homogeneous.

Then Sam thought of examining it under the microscope. He found that it was full of microscopic bubbles—hollow places! By later experiment, we found that the metal was just a sponge of the strange alloy, filled with tiny bubbles of helium gas, under considerable pressure. Sam presently formulated the theory that the alloy, when formed, had contained considerable amounts of radium compounds; and that the alpha particles, or charged helium atoms, thrown off by the disintegration of the radium, while the metal was in a semi-plastic state, had been imprisoned in it.

But it was not until later—much later—that we got the true meaning of it—that we understood the insidious force that acted in the metal, to make human beings slaves to it!

So the days went by—happy, carefree days for me. I knew real joy for the first time in my life. Since youth I had known the Green Girl in my fancy. I had longed to find her, with a restless, hopeless longing that had left me discontented and unhappy, whatever my surroundings. Now, at last, she was really mine. I loved her with a singleness and intensity of affection that turned all my emotion in one direction, so I felt little fear or care for anything else.

One day, when we sat like children together on a cool, moss-covered rock beneath a great fragrant purple tree, with a crystal pool before us, gleaming like molten ruby in the light of the scarlet sky, I told her quite simply that I loved her— that I had known her always, and loved her as long.

"The white chieftain of my dreams," she whispered, "for what long years I have wished for you to come and tell me that…"

There was no need for further words between us. It was a long, long time before we returned to the machine, and then I am afraid we both flushed a little before the smile of tender understanding on Sam's lean face.

CHAPTER TWENTY-FIVE
The Tragedy in the Purple Wood

OUR WOODLAND LIFE was happy. We were quite unconscious of the events that were shaping themselves to bring sudden catastrophe. We saw in our simple lives no foreshadowing of the supreme moments of the stupendous drama in which we were involved. The crisis came with little enough warning.

On the last day of our joyous existence there (we had fallen into the habit of making an arbitrary division of our time into days and nights), Sam arose and fixed our breakfast. I remember that we had pancakes, with maple syrup. Then, since "Alexander" was fluttering about, eager for the day's hunt, and flickering messages to him with its petal-like membrane, he got his rifle and they departed.

As the old scientist walked off through the purple trees, puffing steadily on the old pipe in his mouth, fondly watching the huge, winged beast that flew along above him with his gun, little did I dream of the tragedy that was in store! I could not have believed that Sam stood in any great danger. The winged creature that attended him was two-thirds grown; it would have been more than a match for a couple of lions! Certainly it was no feeble bodyguard!

An hour after he had gone, Xenora and I took one of my old romances of science, and walked a quarter of a mile up the limpid stream to a favorite resort of ours. We laughed and talked much by the way, and gathered a great bunch of the little red blooms. I was teaching her to read—at least that was our nominal business, though it was usually forgotten.

The living, wonderful mystery of her, her sheer perfection, the life and love that sparkled in her eyes, all enchanted me, carried my thoughts away from the page!

We sat together on our mossy stone seat, reading a little, and laughing and talking much, until we forgot all except each other. When I looked at my watch, I found that we had been there many hours. We got up and started back to the machine, speculating light-heartedly on what Sam would have ready for dinner.

We shouted carefree greetings as we approached the machine, and received no reply. We got to the deck, and descended to the cabin in vague alarm, but saw no sign of the old scientist. We hoped that he had only been delayed. I blew the siren several times, and listened to hear a signal from his gun. But when the echoes of the blast had died away from the silent purple wood, all was still again. We heard no answering shot.

I climbed out on the deck to listen. Not a sound disturbed the stillness, save the faint rustle of the unceasing wind in the purple trees above, and the crystal tinkle of the little stream. Green meadows and bright trees lay steaming beneath the hot red sky—quiet as death. The stillness was ominous. It bore the portent of doom!

Presently Xenora crept up by me and ran her strong cool arm through mine. Her violet eyes were solemn, now; and her fair face was clouded with anxiety. She had come to share my love for Sam.

"I am afraid for him," she whispered. "Many things might have happened. The beasts he hunted may have charged and killed him. Or a ship of Mutron may have found him—the ships of the Lord of Flame travel even to the waters of the lower sea to do battle with the Lunaks. And there is another danger of the wood—which is never seen. The hunters of Lothar never venture far from the city."

Her words were not particularly encouraging, and I made ready to go to look for Sam at once. I carried a heavy rifle, my pistol, and an emergency medicine kit. Xenora insisted on going along, and I could do nothing but assent. I did not wish to leave her alone, and she herself was no mean woodsman. In fact, when it came to the matter of following the trail over the low green plants, she proved far more expert than myself.

We left at once. The trail led us east for a mile, parallel to the stream, in the cover of the purple trees. Then it turned north across an open meadow; and there Xenora picked up the spoor of one of the great sloths, which Sam had stalked. It led on to a group of three giant purple trees, and there we found two fired cartridges from Sam's rifle. Three hundred yards farther on, in an open meadow, we found the kill.

Alexander had evidently had his fill from it; and near by were the dying embers of a fire, and the charred green stick on which Sam had cooked a steak for himself. The ground around the fire was somewhat torn up. The green plants had been uprooted and crushed. And there on the ground I found another cartridge from the rifle.

Presently Xenora picked up a trail leading toward a clump of the flowering trees to the north. We followed it hastily, silent with fearful anticipations. Twice we saw on the ground great splashes of green liquid, of the life-fluid of the plant creatures. Had Sam's pet been fighting for him in the air as he fled?

Then we came to the pitiful end of the trail. The ground was frightfully torn up, as if great bodies had struggled there. There were great splotches of the green fluid, and a fateful stain—evidently of human blood. Sam's battered pith helmet we found on the ground there, and six fired shells—silent tokens of the battle!

From the spot no trail led away. There was no evidence to show whether the battle had ended in death or in capture, nor anything to show what manner of being the unknown assailant had been. For a long time we stood there, gazing at the spot in lifeless grief and despair, apathetically fingering the helmet and shells, vainly trying to picture the contest, and looking about for other signs.

"It is no use to go farther," Xenora said at last. "It is the unknown menace of the purple wood. Many a man of Lothar has been taken by it—it is a silent, winged death."

CHAPTER TWENTY-SIX
The Last City of Lothar

PRESENTLY WE turned and trudged wearily back to the Omnimobile. There was nothing else to do. I was sick with an aching heart. It was incredible that Sam, kind and true friend that he had always been, should be no more. A choking lump rose in my throat, and I confess that a few tears rolled down my cheek.

But I still had Xenora. As we walked, I put my arms around her, protectingly, in the grim determination that this strange world should not rob me also of the dream girl for whom I had searched two worlds. My love of her kept me from utter despair, but even then I knew that our ideal life could not go on.

I would have to find what it was that had taken Sam—to identify the thing that Xenora called so vaguely "the menace of the purple wood." Might it be the wild plant monsters, or was it something even more alien and terrible? And I thought more seriously of the danger to the Earth, which I had been trying so vainly to forget. Sam's responsibility had fallen on my shoulders. I must see what I could do.

With the wonderful intuitive knowledge of one another's thoughts that Xenora and I have always had, she understood what was passing in my mind before I said anything. Softly, she took my fingers in her hand, and looked at me with deep sympathy in her eyes.

"I know, Melvin, what you think. And it is right. It is hard, so soon after you have come here to find me—but it must be. I can guide you to the city of my people. I can even show you to the brink of the pit of Xath, if you would go there!"

"You are very brave and true, my princess."

"I come from Lothar! If you feel that your duty bids you risk the violet death in Xath, I would not dissuade you. But the Lord of Flame is mighty—no man can fight him. He has power over all!"

"Except our love," I said. I stopped, and took her in my arms, and pressed her red warm lips against my own. In the whole world, she was all that was mine. She clung to me fiercely, as if the terrible power of the pit of flames was trying to tear her away.

At last we went on, and presently we reached the Omnimobile, hidden in the purple grove. In Sam's absence, it looked very cheerless and lonely. We got aboard and made ready for departure. I tuned up the motors, and examined the electric weapons, and cleaned and loaded the little cannon again. As I worked, Xenora went in the galley and fixed a lunch. We ate quickly, under the silent pall of bitter tragedy, thinking of the smiling old man that should have been with us.

Then we climbed into the conning tower, and I switched on the engines. The humming of the generators rose again, and the great machine lumbered clumsily out of the little wood, where it had been hidden for so many happy days. For many hours we held a northwestward course over the green plateaus and through the purple woodlands, with the light of the crimson day shining through the ports.

Xenora stood by me and chose the route. For the last few miles we crept along just east of a high, bare ridge of rocks. At last she bade me stop the machine in a clump of trees at the foot of the hill. The last city of Lothar, she said, lay but a mile beyond.

I took my binoculars and a rifle, and we left the machine and clambered up a half mile to the top of the ridge. The girl led the way, slipping cautiously through the rocks. At last she threw herself down behind a fringe of the low green plants, and motioned me to crawl up beside her.

"Look," she whispered, "and see all that is left of Lothar, the proud kingdom of my fathers, under the curse of the Lord of Flame!" Indeed it was a scene of ruined grandeur that met my eyes. A little valley, perhaps two miles wide, lay beyond the ridge on which we were concealed. On the low hill beyond, standing out against the crimson sky, was a massive ruined wall. Back of it rose the crumbling desolate ruins of great towers and palaces of stone, covered with the moss of centuries of decay—merely the bare bleached skull of a dead civilization.

"It was in those fallen palaces of my fathers," Xenora whispered again, "that I found the strange machine that brought me the first dream of you."

I put up the glasses and made out the actual city outside the wall. Certainly Lothar had fallen since its days of radio. There was a mere straggling village of rude stone huts spread out on the valley floor, below the colossal ruined metropolis. The few hundred buildings were surrounded by a little cleared space, with the purple forest creeping up to reclaim it forever. I made out a few children playing about the trees, and a dozen ill-clad men working in the clearings. A few wreaths of smoke curled up from the dwellings; the people had not yet lost the art of fire.

And hanging silent and menacing in the air above the village was the visible symbol of the alien power that had wrecked that ancient civilization! A great, gleaming silver ball—a ship like the one we had fought—hung motionless above the huts, with a quick purple beam from it flickering frequently over them!

For a long time we lay there watching that desolate, pitiful scene, and then Xenora touched my arms, and we slipped back down the ridge. She was silent, with grief and despair in her eyes.

"See…" she whispered at last. "See. Lothar is dead! The Lord of Flame has killed it. The men are poor struggling wretches; they could do nothing even if the flame were gone. My father was the last king of Lothar. His was a troubled reign, and he has been dead many hundred sleeps."

"Don't grieve so, my princess," I said; "There are still vast cities above the waters, where men are powerful and wise, and where the sky is blue and a white sun shines, and where there is a domain many times larger than all this abyss."

"Can we go there—ever?" she questioned eagerly.

"No. We can never leave this land, even if the Lord of Flame is killed. The machine cannot break through the roof of water from below. And the power of the Lord of Flame is coming to Earth. Even now it may be a dead and frozen world."

And drooping in the silence of dull despair, we reached the machine, and drove quickly for the protection of the deeper wood.

CHAPTER TWENTY-SEVEN
Mutron of the Sleepers

FOR HALF A DOZEN hours we lumbered eastward through the forest. We wallowed through swamps, and rolled over broad green meadows alight with the crimson day, and broke through jungles bright with purple bloom. At last we emerged on a narrow upland, with the great lake below it. The black sheet of water, tinged with the red light of the sky, stretched away for many miles to the eastward. Along its northern shore we could see the low cliffs that divided it from the pit of Xath.

We stopped the machine, and looked for a long time across the black lake to the north, and over the low cliffs to the ruby mist beyond, alive with the dancing violet lights.

Then I turned to the rare girl beside me, who was watching me with tears brimming in her violet eyes. The utter grief, the black despair on her face half broke my resolution. I felt doubtful, weak, utterly miserable, with pain stabbing at my heart like a thin steel blade.

"It is right. You must go," she whispered bravely.

I took her in my arms again. How wonderful and true she was! Struggling so bravely to hold back her tears. More precious than ever in the final parting. A single hour of the heaven of that embrace—embittered by the knowledge that it would soon be ended!

Then, quickly, lest my resolution fail, I made ready for departure. I stretched up a tent in a little grove above the lake, and stocked it with a liberal assortment of supplies from our storeroom. I gave Xenora an automatic and a case of ammunition, and showed her how to use the weapon. Here she was to stay, in the vain hope that I might return a victor from the mad attack on the Lord of Flame.

For I had determined to enter the abyss. I knew that was what Sam would have me do, rather than lose time in an attempt to learn his fate. Xenora was eager to cast her lot with mine, but I would not hear of it.

A choking lump was in my throat as I staggered aboard the Omnimobile, and closed the manhole with a trembling hand. I gave a final heartbreaking glance to the splendid girl, majestic and erect, even in her pain, standing desolate and alone by the tent. Then I turned on the generators, and drove north along the lakeshore.

I had the rude map that Sam had drawn from Xenora's knowledge. It showed the pit of the Lord of Flame to be just north of the lake, separated from it only by a surprisingly narrow wall of cliffs which, the girl said, had been a highway of her fathers, though it was now covered with jungle. And the city of Mutron was shown north of me, on the brink of the pit of Xath.

Steadily I drove northward, in a daze of fevered pain. It seems an eternity when I look back upon it, but it could not have been many hours. Automatically I kept in the shelter of the purple trees. At last I emerged on the edge of a great plateau, covered with the green vegetation, many miles across. On the south and west, from whence I had come, it was surrounded by purple trees—by the thick purple wood in which I had halted. On the north the great cliffs towered up to the sharp-edged scarlet roof, four miles above. It was strange to see the blue walls cut off so abruptly by the red. The sky was like a red lake seen inverted in a mirror. Those blue cliffs were hardly a dozen miles away now—I had to bend back my head to see the sharp line where the roof cut them off.

On the east side of that plateau, there was—nothing!

Beyond, lay the pit of Xath, with the faint ruby mist above it, filled as always with the wavering reflections of violet flames. And a half dozen miles before me, on the brink of that pit, stood—Mutron!

The City of the Sleepers!

A strange scene it was. A city of silver metal! Domes and towers and pyramids of argent whiteness! Vast incredible machines! Huge and oddly wrought structures! Titanic cubes and cylinders and cones! All of gleaming silver The city shone with a cold light. It was as weird, as unearthly, as a dead city of the moon. It had the silent, ghostly gleam of moonlight. It was wrapped in mystery, clad in frozen fear!

And the city was not idle. Those vast amazing machines were moving. Silver globe-ships were drifting in silent haste above it. And ever and anon, one of them dropped over the rim, into the pit of Xath, or one floated unexpectedly up out of that abyss!

As I stood there in the Omnimobile, in the shadow of the last of the purple trees, my heart grew sick again with doubt. What, indeed, could I, with my puny machine, do against the great science that that city of mystery represented? The men of one once mighty empire were now slaves to it. What hope was there for me? Was not the human race, like the bison or the dodo, about to fall before a superior power?

But there would be no turning back. I saw to it that all the machinery was in order, and returned to the conning tower. Before me was the instrument board that controlled the electric arc and the rocket tubes, as well as the machinery.

I started the hydrodyne generators at their full capacity, and then threw the switch. As the half million horsepower went through the resistance coils, jets of super-heated steam roared out of the nozzles, condensing in white rushing clouds. The terrific force of the jets uprooted the purple trees, and the machine vibrated to the mighty blast. I was hurled into the air. With a speed that swiftly increased to many hundreds of miles per hour, I hurtled the broad plain, and over the ghostly white city of silver—and into the abyss!

The plateau ended abruptly as if cut off with a knife. The crater fell sheer away before me, stretching to the vast blue cliffs in the north and to the line of living purple and green that marked the beginning of the eastward forests. Only a thin green line separated the abyss from the lake on the south, which, in the reflected light of the scarlet sky, horribly suggested a sea of blood, ready to flow into the pit.

Undoubtedly the crater was of volcanic origin. I could not determine its depth, nor the state of its floor—it was filled with the thick crimson mist. The wavering tongues of violet fire still flickered through it, throbbing strangely, like the reflection of fires below—hinting unpleasantly of alien life.

As the rich green plain vanished beneath me, and I sped high over that busy strange white city and into the haze of the abyss, an odd feeling of the wildness and the unfamiliar terror of the place stole over me again. I was very thankful for the invention of Sam's, for the thin helmet of wire gauze above my head!

Suddenly a great twisting bar of green fire writhed up, like a serpent's head, from the nest of flames. It swung and coiled and twisted through the rosy mists with a slow, deliberate motion, like an incredible reptile of flame raising its head, looking, searching! Despite the helmet, great fear swept my brain like a hot flame!

CHAPTER TWENTY-EIGHT
The Flaming Brain

MIGHTY WINDS whipped about me. The roaring jets of steam drove the throbbing machine on over the rosy mists, and over the flickering violet flames. And I fell—dropped into the hidden pit. Vividly I saw the great writhing head of green rising above the fire-fog ahead, with that in its waving, serpentine motion that told me that its eyes were already upon me! I was certain that it was a living, sentient entity, that it was intelligent!

Could my weapons avail against it?

I fell through the rosy clouds. The green and purple rim of the abyss grew vague, and the blue cliffs in the north assumed a misty indistinctness. The red mist shone until it seemed that I was swimming in a fog of crimson fire.

And all the while the bright beautiful face of Xenora was before me. The light of her clear violet eyes drove the strangeness and the fear from my mind, leaving only my pain at leaving her. I drove the machine mechanically, lost in a daze of grief.

For ages, it seemed, I shot forward through the haze. At last I made out a bare floor of sand and rocks, pitted with circular craters. It was a good thousand feet below, and still dim in the haze. I opened the bow tubes, and the force of my fall was checked. In three minutes more, the machine struck the earth, bow first. It tore a vast hole in the sand, and rolled over twice, coming to rest on its side. Fortunately it had been built to withstand such knocks; fortunately, too, I was strapped in my cushioned seat.

I got the motors started and worked the machine to an upright position. The crater floor was visible for half a mile about in all directions. It was a dead, desolate waste of hard sand and twisted black volcanic rocks. Further vision was cut off by the rosy mist that hung above the floor.

Then I saw, far before me, a bright violet gleam through the crimson mist. Indistinctly I saw a broad green shaft of pulsing fire rise from it, to lose itself in the crimson sky. That intense violet light, from which the flickering reflections came, and from which the green beam reached up, I knew, must be the seat of the Lord of Flame!

I started the engines once more, and the machine rolled mightily forward over the bare rocks, with a great clangor of metal upon stone, forging ahead at last to meet the alien menace. It roared over bare sandy flats, rounded great boulders, crashed into pits, crawled through craters. Then, suddenly, that terrible green flame flared out toward me! I knew that I had been discovered! Like a lance of green flame it flashed through the red gloom above. Its motion was alert, surprised, terrible.

I set the loading mechanism of the little gun to fire high explosive, and put it in action, hurling shells in the direction of that violet light. And still I drove swiftly on. The flashes of the explosions were visible through the mist ahead, but the deep violet light still glowed.

I turned on the reserve power units, and the machine vibrated from their throbbing drone. I threw another switch, and the deep purr of the giant transformers filled the ship. The mighty white tongue of the electric arc reached out ahead of me!

And the Omnimobile plunged on!

Two of the silver spheres—the ships of Mutron—appeared before me, with the green vortexes of the atomic disintegration springing up about them. The great arc brought them down in incandescent wreckage almost as soon as they came into view!

The violet mist grew brighter, more distinct. I knew the shells were bursting near it, and that the arc would reach it soon. The faithful old machine lumbered rapidly on over the wild and twisted rocky desert—a waste as terrible as the mountains of the moon.

In fact, that crater-pitted floor bore a curious resemblance to the typical lunar landscape, and the forces that produced them must have been similar.

Then the mist cleared, and I saw the form of the thing that gave the violet light! It was scores of feet thick, and hundreds tall. It was a vast smooth cylinder of violet fire! It shone like metal, which was white hot and seen through violet glass. The color of it ran and flickered on the surface. Violet sheets and bands crawled and flashed upon it, and violet flame flowed away from it in many little tongues. The thing was perfectly smooth and cylindrical, five hundred feet in height—a titanic "monolith" of metal!

Still the Omnimobile lumbered irresistibly onward. The little gun crashed regularly, and the shells threw up the earth about that weird cylinder half a mile ahead. And the great white flame of the arc was playing far out toward it like the sword of the angel of death!

I saw a cluster of curious gleaming machines about the base of the great cylinder. One of my shells must have struck them, for they suddenly seemed to collapse and dissolve in a cloud of white smoke.

Abruptly a huge, terrible bar of green fire rose from the top of the cylinder almost like an extension of it—it was like a beam of green light from a vast searchlight. But it bent and twisted, as if it were alive. It moved like a snake, writhed toward me!

And then came the catastrophe!

A great pit in the rocky desert suddenly appeared before me—a hundred-foot chasm! I made a wild attempt to swing the machine around it. But, busy with the arc, the generators, and the gun, I had seen it too late. The brink loomed before me! Desperately I set the brakes. The machine paused jerkily, hesitated, then leaped over the rim! For a breathless second it fell down the sheer crater wall! I had no time to use the rockets. It crashed heavily upon the rocks!

I was torn from my seat and flung cruelly against the side of the conning tower. My helmet was knocked off. And on the instant, a red storm of fear broke about me! It beat down on my brain like a rain of horror. It throbbed with an archaic rhythm, stirring strange emotions that overruled my reason and volition. Terror swept about me like a fierce wind from a hot desert of death, picking up my soul and sweeping it away to a fate unnamable!

I struggled with it terribly, with all my will. But it beat down my feeble barriers like a resistless tide. It burned away my will like a hot flame in my brain!

That horror came over me in a vast, overwhelming wave! It seized my body! My hand moved unwillingly, and cut off the current of the great arc! And then my body was struggling to its feet, opening the manhole, and clambering out of the machine. But still the thing did not have *me!* I was still an independent entity that sat apart and watched.

I knew that I had succumbed to the hypnotic control of the alien power that dwelt in that vast metal cylinder. I was another of the slaves of the Lord of Flame—of the Sleepers of Mutron!

CHAPTER TWENTY-NINE
Xenora's Sacrifice

I WAS MOVED OUT of the machine like an automaton by the terrible force that controlled me. My body was no longer my own. It was swept along as if by a mighty wind. That force of horror roared and throbbed in my brain. Red flames of fear flickered before my eyes. I was sick and faint with terror. But my body did not collapse—it was relentlessly moved by that terrible force from the violet cylinder. I was utterly helpless—I felt the hopeless horror of one chained before a loathsome monster!

Suddenly I wished fiercely for death, for only death could bring me freedom from the horror that swept in a throbbing torrent through my brain. But even death was beyond my reach, for my hands were not my own!

For a moment that power left me standing on the side of the overturned machine. The Omnimobile lay on the sandy floor of the crater, which may have been a hundred feet in depth and as many yards across. Against the red sky, above the black cliffs of the pit's farther rim, towered the violet metal cylinder—the flaming metal brain whose hypnotic control ruled my body.

For a moment I was left standing there, and then my body was springing down and running across the rock-strewn sand toward the cliffs. It ran like a machine—beyond my control! In vain I tried even to stumble and fall. In a few moments it reached the rim. It clambered wildly up. I know that in my normal self I could never have surmounted that sheer wall. But the telepathic force from the flaming brain seemed to give my limbs superhuman strength. Soon I was at the top, with bleeding hands and tattered clothing.

And my body ran on toward the violet monostyle!

It was two hundred yards away—a titanic smooth upright cylinder of metal, the polished surface crawling and flowing with violet flame, with the great incredible serpent-like beam of green rising from the top.

It was astounding—in the strangeness of its aspect, and in its inexplicable suggestion of alien intelligence. But how could there be intelligence in metal?

And then I saw the men about it!

Two of the vast silver spheres were stopped on the ground below the cylinder, oddly dwarfed by its vast height. And about them were men. They were the green slaves—the Sleepers of Mutron! Their bodies were naked but for tattered scraps of cloth. Fastened upon their backs by the cruel metal clamps, they bore the strange prisms!

But those bars of metal were not blue like the one we had taken from the dead man. They shone with the same mysterious violet radiance as the titanic monostyle. They were parts of it—akin to it!

The men moved like sleepers, or like machines, as I felt that I was moving—as if their wills were dead. They toiled in tireless haste, without confusion. Many were carrying burdens. And it seemed that some were polishing the surface of the cylinder, or applying some luminous substance to it. Near the ground they were quite plainly visible, clinging to its surface like flies, and toiling furiously. Higher up on the colossal cylinder they were but dancing black specks within the violet flame.

The ground about was pitted with shell holes from my bombardment, and at one side I saw the twisted wreck of the great machine I had struck. It is possible that I had hit the great cylinder itself, but it might have received the fire of the biggest gun in Christendom with little injury.

In two minutes more I had been drawn to within fifty yards of that vast shining column of metal. Then the force of fear that had seized my body permitted it to stop, and I stood still. That awful twisting beam of green flame reached out of the top of the thing, and bent down over me. It touched me!

I felt tiny whip-like fingers of it feeling—exploring my body! The green radiance grew denser about me. It enshrouded me in a fog of green light—so painfully intense, blinding and terrible, that I tried to shut my eyes against it. But that horror held them open!

And that green fire came into my body, and into my brain. It was eager, insistent, questioning—and so horrible that my being rocked with pain. It questioned; it commanded! It sought to know of me, and of my companions, of the Omnimobile, and of the world we had left above. I struggled against it, fiercely, terribly, until I felt my limbs chilling with the sweat of the conflict. But it won!

It took my mind as it had taken my body. It beat about my brain like a vast storm; it penetrated my being in a flood of green fire. My brain reeled, was swept by an avalanche of awful power. I sank at last into merciful oblivion that was the counterpart of the death I had so desired!

At last, when I was vaguely conscious again, I had a curious feeling of mental exhaustion. I felt as if I had undergone a fearful ordeal. I felt as if I had toiled as I slept, as if I had answered many questions put to me by that power. It seemed as if the green light had swept the contents from my brain, had searched all my knowledge.

As I awoke, bodily sensation returned, and I felt someone lifting me gently from the bare earth upon which I lay. My limbs were cold and stiff; but the awful force that had controlled them was, for the moment, relaxed.

I opened my eyes, and cried out, first in incredulous joy, and then in utter despair. Xenora—the Green Girl—was lifting my head. There was anxiety and care in her violet eyes, and unutterable fatigue was shown in her body. She had followed me into the pit, to give her life with mine!

"Oh, Xenora, my dream girl, why did you come? There was no need for you to give your life," I protested in bitter despair as she raised me in her arms and held me against her breast.

"I felt you battle with the Lord of Flame. I felt it conquer you. So I left the camp, to come."

"And how, in all wonders, did you get into this pit, and so soon?"

"My chieftain, it is not so soon. For three sleeps I have come through the forests and rocks, without stopping, while you lay still in the power of the Flame!"

"But why—why—come to throw away your life—"

"See, I bring you the wonderful thing of Barsoni Sam, that shuts out the horror. I give it to you, and you can go on with your battle against the Flame!—No, you can never conquer the Flame! But fly. Go back to your land!"

Even then I felt the horror awakening again, felt that fearful force directed again upon me. With a single quick motion, before I could prevent her, Xenora had whipped the electro-screen helmet from her head and drawn it about my own.

"Fly," she whispered fiercely. "The Sleepers of Mutron! And think not of me. Fly! Even from me!"

The horror relaxed, and I collapsed in a daze of relief. In a moment I had recovered and got to my feet. Xenora was a score of yards away, dashing off. I ran after her, calling for her to take back the precious helmet.

Suddenly she stopped. A convulsion ran through her frame.

She turned, with her face a mask of livid horror. She was in the power of the Flame! She was a Sleeper! She bent, seized a rock, and hurled it at my head with superhuman strength. I dodged and it hurtled past my ear. She sprang at me like an animal, drawing the hunting knife I had left her.

I turned and ran wildly, as a score of the Sleepers came running. I passed close by that violet metal monostyle, and it seemed that its crawling violet fires reached out for me. I ran desperately toward the east. I heard the strange cries of the Sleepers of Mutron behind me! I felt the awful green flame writhing above me, but even it could not penetrate the helmet.

I was insane with terror!

I ran on and on, through eternities of heart-breaking effort.

At last I stopped exhausted, with pounding temples and bursting lungs, to look behind me. The flaming brain was but a dull violet glow against the red sky. A desolate waste of bare rugged rocks and great round craters lay about me beneath the crimson mist. All was silent. The sounds of pursuit were gone!

CHAPTER THIRTY
The Nitrate Foundation

SHOULD I GO ON, or return and try to save Xenora, as she had rescued me? The question throbbed in my brain. The answer would have been easy enough if I had had her alone to consider. I might cheerfully have surrendered myself to that dreaded power to save her—any man would have done as much! But what of the menace to the Earth? Should I give up the struggle?

For a long time I stood there on the rim of a strange crater, lost in indecision. At last my sense of duty to mankind was victor. I set off wearily toward the east again. The Omnimobile was so near the flaming brain that I dared not attempt to reach it, even if I had been confident of finding it. And upon consideration, I was sure that if the machine was left as it was, it would be only as a trap for me.

A sorry hope, indeed, was I for victory in the struggle with that vast alien power for the safety of Earth. A man alone, ragged, without even a pocketknife, lost in the wilderness of a strange world, and possessing only a modicum of scientific knowledge.

What folly, indeed, for one in such circumstances to pit himself against such a science. But that seemed the only hope for victory. With Sam in my place, the outlook would have been brighter. If I had a fair scientific education, Sam knew enough to raise cities and armies in the wilderness!

For many hours I struggled toward the east—away from the violet glow—over the desert of rocks and craters, through the ruby mist. And I came unexpectedly upon an explanation for the origin of the crimson haze. Thin clouds of red luminous gas were hissing from some of the craters or funaroles—escaping from the radium deposits in the core of the Earth, to float up and augment the radioactive cloud that held up the waters!

I was half-dead with weariness when I reached the mile-high cliffs at the crater's rim, and half-insane with grief for Xenora, and with angry doubt of my wisdom in deserting her. I have little memory of how I got up that wall of rocks. I remember climbing until I was worn out, of toiling upward with bleeding hands and feet, of fighting on when I was dizzy for want of food and water, of struggling up when my body screamed in pain for me to surrender and drop to merciful oblivion in the abyss. I remember sleeping many times on ledges or in crevices when I could go no farther.

But at last I reached the rim.

I climbed out upon the flat plateau to the east of the abyss, a strange wilderness of green plains and purple trees, but infinitely welcome after the tortures through which I had been. I stumbled across the meadows until I found a little stream. Eagerly I wet my parched mouth, and presently I slaked my thirst, and ate a few of the date-like fruits of the flowering trees. And then I slept.

For a period of many months thereafter, I led a strange wild life—the life of a beast or a savage. It now seems to me that I must have been more than half-insane, yet I had cunning of a sort. Wandering about in the woodland in the first few days, before my strength was fully recovered, I came upon a great lump of native copper. With hammer and anvil of stone I set out to shape some tools of it. First I made a knife, and then a broad blade for a wooden spear. With those weapons I soon had stalked and killed one of the great fat sloths. After several weary efforts, I achieved a fire by friction, and feasted upon roasted meat.

Many were the mad and impossible schemes that my fevered brain formed for making an attack on the flaming brain of metal, only to reject each upon consideration. As I had hurtled through the air above the pit, in my ill-starred attack in the Omnimobile, I had been much impressed by the narrowness of the bridge of cliffs between the great lake and the abyss. Now it occurred to me that I might dig a canal, and let the waters of the lake in to flood the Lord of Flame.

With that in mind, I made an expedition to the isthmus, armed with copper pick and spade. I found that my eyes had curiously deceived me, from the air. The land bridge was a wall of rock, nowhere less than a hundred feet high and four hundred thick, covered with a rank growth of jungle. Along it, even as Xenora had said, was a ruined road. Here and there a crumbling stone monument rose from the jungle like a bleached skull of the dead civilization.

There was no hope of digging a canal. A hundred men, in ten years, might have been able to cut a tunnel through that wall of stone, with modern tools and explosives.

Nitroglycerin!

That started me on a new line of thought. I had once made chemistry a hobby. It was not impossible. For Sam, it would have been child's play. But alas, there was no help from my old friend.

I set to work at once. For many months I labored. The task was a tremendous one. The first necessity was an adequate supply of nitrates. I was not fortunate enough to discover a natural deposit, as heroes of fiction usually are; so I set out to make a "nitrate plantation" such as is used for the manufacture of nitrates in a primitive way. I dug a great shallow pit, lined it with waterproof clay, and filled it with alternate layers of wood ashes obtained by burning the purple trees, and everything I could pick up in the way of nitrogenous animal and vegetable refuse. At last it was filled and wet down with water from my daybed. I had nothing to do but wait until the nitrogen products of decomposition had united themselves with the potassium bases in the wood ashes.

Then I fell to the mining of iron pyrites, and to the building of a furnace in which I could burn my pottery apparatus. After many disheartening failures I was able to set up apparatus that I thought would suffice for the manufacture of my acids. I burned rude jars, glazed with sand, in which to carry and store my reagents and explosives.

My memory of all that time is a dim dream of terror. Many times for long hours I stood on the brink, gazing into the flickering mist, thinking intently of Xenora and half determined to give it all up and to seek her. But always I went back to my mad task, toiling in a daze of grief and despair.

Before I did anything more in the way of manufacture, I paid another visit to the isthmus, and selected the site for the mine that was to tear an opening in it. I found a deep crevice in the rocks, and spent many weeks in clearing and enlarging it, until I had ready a chamber deep in the heart of the barrier, below the level of the lake.

During all that time I lived upon the little fruits and upon the flesh of the sloths I killed. I carefully saved the fat from the latter, saponified it with alkalis leached from wood ashes, and removed the soap by "salting down" with evaporated brine from a salt spring. I collected and stored the glycerin until I had many gallons.

At last, judging that my "nitrate plantation" had had time to serve its purpose, I dug it up, leached the product, and crystallized the saltpeter by evaporation in earthen pots. The yield was satisfactory in quantity and fair in quality, but it had cost fearful effort.

Then I set about the manufacture of sulfuric acid by roasting the iron pyrites with nitrate in my crude apparatus, collecting the acid in a number of wet pottery condensers. That took many days, and the next step was making nitric acid by boiling saltpeter in sulfuric acid and condensing the fumes.

At last, when I had the three necessary chemicals— glycerin, and nitric and sulfuric acids—I set out to transport them separately to my mine, to avoid the hazard of the transportation of the finished product. That, again, was a heartbreaking task, for I had materials enough to make several hundred quarts of nitroglycerin, and the distance was half a dozen miles.

But ragged, ill-kept savage that I was, I had collected on the cliffs above my shaft the materials for the manufacture of a good quantity of high explosive. For one in my position, it had been a considerable achievement.

CHAPTER THIRTY-ONE
The Mine on the Brink

AT LAST, IN HASTE and fear and trembling, I began the task of mixing my chemicals, dumping them into vats of water cooled by evaporation, under a rude shed to cut off the fierce heat of the red sky. Even with all my precautions to prevent a premature explosion, the hazard was fearful. I washed the nitroglycerin, and carried it in earthen jars down into the heart of the cliffs. I meant to die in the final explosion, but I was afraid the stuff would go off before it was in place.

But finally I got the last of the rough jars into position. Then I closed the mouth of the chamber with rocks and rubbish, to be sure that the full force of the explosion would be exerted upon the cliff. I lit the fuse I had prepared—a tall candle of the sloth's fat, which, burning low, would ignite a powder train; and that would set off a charge of gunpowder I had placed by the jars of nitroglycerin.

I knew that, if my terrible months of toil had not been in vain, a few hours more would see a raging torrent of water rushing into the pit. At last I judged my task completed. I walked a few yards north to the rim. I stood on the brink of that sheer precipice, and gazed down into the rosy mist, alight, as always, with the wavering, reflected fires of the metal brain. I made no attempt to get beyond the range of the explosion. Hope was dead. Life meant no more to me. I was ready to be swept into the abyss on the crest of the wave that, if my plans went well, would drown the flaming brain.

For a long time I stood there waiting, lost in dreams of Xenora. I had no doubt that she was dead. My regret was bitter; I stormed vainly and passionately at fate. If my reason had been tottering, now it was almost gone. I wept, and cursed, and then laughed loud and bitterly. A strange figure I must have been, wild and unkempt, red and burned from exposure, half-naked, with insanity in my eyes, laughing and waiting to be blown to my doom!

And then I heard a sound that brought me into silent and cunning alertness! I sprang to the mouth of my shaft and crouched like a savage with my great copper-bladed spear at hand. I heard a stone rattling and crashing down into the abyss! Someone—or something—was climbing up out of the pit! I crept forward where I could see, and lay tense and silent, a desperate madman, determined to protect my mine against whatever might find it.

At last a human figure clambered up over the brink, and drew itself erect in the edge of the jungle! It was a Sleeper of Mutron! The emaciated form was bent beneath the weight of the bar of gleaming violet metal clamped upon its back. It was clad in tattered, bloody rags. The flesh was bleeding from the fearful climb.

With the dull, mechanical motions of a sleeping person, or of a walking corpse, galvanized by some weird power, that terrible figure got deliberately to its feet. The bloody hands raised a long, glittering weapon of silver metal. And it plodded dully, lifelessly, toward me. And then a hoarse, wild cry echoed through the silent jungle—my own scream!

The Sleeper was Xenora!

With her old intuition of my thoughts, she had been able to penetrate my helmet! Through her, the Lord of Flame had read my thoughts of victory! She had been sent to prevent the mine's explosion, to snuff out that candle flame!

If she heard my scream, she paid no heed. She walked on toward me, with the same weary, mechanical gait. There was no light, no life in her eyes. They stared straight ahead, dully, unseeing! And the strange silver tube was held ready in her hand. She was more like a moving corpse—a dead avenger—than a living person!

A mad storm of desires arose in my brain. How I longed to spring up, to take that dear body in my arms, to minister to its hurts, to have the Green Girl for my own again! It took all my will to hold me in my hiding place. But this was not Xenora. It was a Sleeper of Mutron, a slave of the Lord of Flame!

It was a fearful choice before me. But my resolution held. I would carry on if it tore out my heart. With a burning pain in my breast, I ran my fingers over the jagged copper blade, and tensed my muscles for a spring!

Perhaps, after all, we would be better dead.

My madness was gone, but cold, grim determination remained. I knew that I would not hesitate. The silent, sleeping figure of the Green Girl was but a dozen yards from me, and I raised my ragged blade!

Then—a shadow upon the crimson sky. A whisper that grew to a mighty roar! The beat of many wings! A strange and ringing cry from the air above! A shouted, imperative, strange-toned command! Sam's well-remembered voice! A rushing sweep of vast green wings before my eyes! A tempest of wind as they beat the air! Xenora snatched up and out of my sight by great red tentacles!

I was petrified in incredulous amazement. It seemed impossible that Sam should be alive. Yet, there had been no definite proof of his death. And, I thought, it must have been Alexander that carried him, and that had swept up Xenora.

In a moment I had aroused myself, and dashed out of my hiding place beneath the purple trees. It was an amazing sight that met my eyes. There were numberless thousands of the flying plants on the wing above! The red sky was flecked with their green wings. In a strange semblance to military order they flew, like fleets of battle-planes. In scores and hundreds they dived and circled, in perfect formation. Many of them, I saw, carried weapons—vast clubs, or huge metal-tipped spears, or heavy stones and masses of metal.

And then a flight of them swept downward again, and I saw Sam, mounted on one that must have been Alexander—though the things all looked alike to me. He was evidently controlling the whole squadron with his shouts and gestures. The old scientist still seemed strong and able.

Then I saw Xenora. She was still in the clutch of the winged steed of Sam's. Even as I looked, the red tentacles tore off the flaming violet prism and hurled it into the abyss.

The weird, amazing creature dived. An incredible thing it was, with its armored brown body as large as a shark's, with the vast flower of the flowing colors about its head, with red tentacles like those of a gigantic scarlet octopus, and with wings like those of a green airplane.

It bore down upon me! A great crimson tentacle reached down and picked me up! I was swept through the air, held lightly in that strange grasp, and lifted until I was face to face with Sam, who sat astride the creature! He reached out his strong brown hand and grasped my own.

"Mel, old man, it's some luck to find you! And what do you think of my army? A couple of the flying dragons captured Alex and me, so I've been making the best of a bad situation. The things are really quite intelligent, and I've been drilling them for months. They're hereditary enemies of the alien civilization, anyhow. There's going to be some fight when we meet the silver ships!" Exultant, joyous triumph rang in his tones. He had not noticed my strange condition.

At last I was sufficiently recovered to speak. "I've got a ton of nitroglycerin in that rock," I stammered. "The lake will be running in the pit in an hour or so." My voice had a curious rusty sound.

"Nitroglycerin! You've been making it, and planting a mine! No wonder you look like a ghost. And how comes Xenora to have that damned metal bar on her?"

Abruptly I broke down into uncontrollable tears of relief and joy. I did not try to answer. In a few minutes the vast army of winged monsters had wheeled about, and was headed north again, over the crimson mists—line after regular line of beating green wings that bore the strangest army of history to the strangest battle ever fought.

But, at the moment, I was paying little attention, for I was mounted on another of those vast flying creatures; and in my arms was Xenora! She was limp, unconscious, sleeping the sleep of utter exhaustion. But she was free again from the Lord of Flame. With tears of joy streaming down my face, I tried to dress her bleeding hands and feet.

CHAPTER THIRTY-TWO
When the Red Roof Fell

ABRUPTLY a green light ran through the rosy haze beneath us, and that dreadful twisting bar of radiance—that living, alien tongue of fire—the serpent-like head of the Lord of Flame, was thrust up out of the flickering violet! With its strange, writhing motion, it swept in a wide arc, as though it saw us. It searched the sky, and then drew back in alarm! The terrible, rhythmic throb of the emerald gleam in it grew faster.

And quickly the crimson sky ahead of our flying army of green-winged monsters was filled with fleets of the silver spheres! They rose swiftly, by the hundred, in long, gleaming lines—floating, drifting, darting, as though carried in swift, cyclonic winds. And then in smoothly sailing squadrons they advanced to meet us, with the swirling green mists of the disintegration force reaching out before them!

The aerial battle-lines met! The winged monsters joined in mad conflict with the silver ships! It was a fierce struggle—a terrible scene! The plant-things swept to the attack, scores in number for each great ship. With desperate, incredible energy they wielded their gigantic clubs and spears; or, wheeling high above the silver vessels, dropped their missiles down upon them.

And the swift searching fingers of purple flame reached out of the silver ships, to guide the thick, swirling vortexes of atomic disintegration. Under that terrible force of flowing green, the plant creatures turned red, battled on for a moment as they glowed with an awful scarlet radiance, and fell in a rain of crimson sparks that fast faded into nothingness!

And ever the throbbing emerald column rising above the sea of ruby mist below us—the writhing serpentine bar of green that was the Lord of Flame—moved and twisted, directing its armies!

The plants battled with desperate ferocity, with incredible strength. In ones and twos and threes, the silver vessels fell, in twisted, battered wreckage—fell among the showers of sparks from the vanished creatures that had crushed them!

It was a battle of animal strength and courage, of desperate, savage energy—against deliberate, inhuman science! It was the battle of the mad, elemental beast—against silent, pitiless power.

And the plants won!

As the monsters that carried Sam and Xenora and myself swept along high above the line of battle, we saw the silver ships give way, saw them drop into the red mist, with the avenging, victorious plants following close upon them.

And then my mine went off!

A vast white cloud of smoke and shattered rock rose deliberately above the cliffs, spread into a Titanic mushroom shape, and fell in a great rain of debris into the abyss and into the lake. After many seconds the sound of it reached us—a crashing, deafening blast! The great wave of air swept up the green-winged fleet like leaves on a stormy lake.

Below the cloud of smoke, where the black cliffs had been, I saw a vast white sheet of waters—a rushing Niagara multiplied manifold—plunging over the brink in a sheer and gleaming arc!

Even as I gazed at it, in dazed wonder at the thing I had wrought, Sam was suddenly close beside me, shouting something with alarm and urgent command in his voice.

"Mel—the roof! Where is the Omnimobile? For God's sake—"

"In a crater in the abyss, by the metal cylinder," I cried, wondering.

Then I looked up, and saw that the flat roof was cupping up, like a vast inverted basin! The waters above were rising!

With no further word to me, Sam shouted a strange order to the monsters we rode. Their vast green wings were folded! We dropped like plummets into the crimson mist! The violet gleam appeared, and we made out the crater-pitted floor. I shouted directions, and in a few minutes we settled into the same little crater in which I had met disaster.

The Omnimobile was still lying there, just as I had left it!

The creatures that bore us dropped near the ground. Those great red tentacles set us gently down on the rocks by the machine. Sam led the way and I carried Xenora.

Desperately we scrambled aboard and screwed down the manhole. Sam's mount, Alexander, slumped into a curious attitude of dejection.

Suddenly one of the silver vessels shot into view above the crater's rim, drifting swiftly towards us! The machine was watched! It had been left as a trap. The thing flashing beams of purple flame reached out eagerly—found the Omnimobile. The whirling spirals of thick green mist extended toward us!

Sam fumbled with the dials and made a hopeless gesture. Then I saw Alexander spring into the air and fly toward the terrible gleaming thing! With mad, desperate speed, the plant creature dashed straight into that fearful swirling mist. It charged on through it! Already glowing red with the disintegration beam, it struck the white machine with terrific force!

The argent globe paused, hung uncertainly, and then fell with swift acceleration until it crashed upon the walls of the pit, with the gleaming, wasting form of the heroic plant still clinging to it in the agony of a fearful doom!

For a long moment Sam was still. Suddenly he aroused himself as if from a daze of pain, and turned again to the instrument boards.

"The Earth is not frozen!" he shouted. "The power in the ether is dead!" I thought of the havoc my cannon fire had wrought with the machines about the flaming brain.

In a moment he had the generators going, and the machine crawling to an upright position. Then he turned on the rocket tubes. The crater was filled with the roaring jets of steam, and we were hurled into the crimson sky!

I had a fleeting glimpse of the metal brain—the vast cylinder of violet—with the green beam still throbbing from it, and with the last of the silver ships battling the victorious army of plants that swarmed about it!

"The roof is lifting!" Sam cried. "The equilibrium was very delicate—the gas that kept issuing from the earth was lifting the waters to the danger point, and your explosion carried them past! The attempt to freeze the Earth was probably undertaken because a roof of ice would have been more secure!"

His voice was drowned in a fresh rushing, whistling burst from the rocket tubes. I carried the inert form of Xenora down to the cabin, and did my best to care for her. In a few moments we were above the haze. I took a last glimpse of the green and purple forests dropping away below us, and turned again to the unconscious girl.

Soon the fierce red glare that poured in the ports told me that we had reached the red roof. And suddenly the Omnimobile was pitching and spinning madly, with wild waters thundering against her sides. A sound reached my ears—a roar, dull, distant and slumberous at first, but rising to a crashing, deafening storm of sound. It seemed an eternity that I held the sleeping girl upon the tossing couch, while the very heavens rocked with thunder!

Abruptly, the bloody glare grew lighter and was streaked with shafts of bright sunshine—white, precious sunlight of the upper Earth! We had followed the vast bubble of gas through the roof of waters. The red mists cleared—drew up into the blue vault above—repelled into outer space!

We were flying in the cold white light, above a mad blue sea!

In fifteen minutes Sam had brought the machine down upon an ocean that was still heaving madly from the cataclysm that had drowned a world. He came into the cabin, and under his skilful ministrations Xenora was soon sleeping quietly, in a normal slumber from which she would wake herself again.

Presently Sam questioned me about my adventures. I gave him the whole account and concluded with the question that, for months, my troubled mind had striven so vainly to answer.

"Sam, how could intelligence exist in metal?"

"Why not in metal, Mel?" the old scientist replied, smiling thoughtfully. "Why not there as well as in lumps of impure carbon and water, as one of the early savants called us? But do you remember the radioactivity of the metal bar, and the little cells of helium gas in it? I think the radium had somehow set up neuronic circuits between the cells, like the circuits between the neuron cells in our brains. It is not impossible. That was a helium brain—but it was formed as naturally as yours or mine."

On May 4, 2000 A. D., just a year after the beginning of my story, our leisurely homeward cruise was ended. The green coast of Florida rose out of the clear blue sea before us. Xenora and I stood on the deck, happy in the cool salty air and the bright sunlight. The girl was lost in vast delight at the new wonders of azure sea and sapphire sky. At last the dream of my life was come true!

The wonderful girl of my fancy was by my side, to be mine forever!

But she was the Green Girl no longer! A week of the sun and wind of the sea had erased the soft green tint of her clear skin, and replaced it with a light, smooth tan!

THE END

HURLED INTO A FUTURE WORLD OF ROBOTS AND HUMAN SLAVES...

Imagine what it would be like to find yourself thrown—unwillingly—into a state of frozen suspended animation. Imagine awakening in a world of the future—a hundred and fifty years later! That's what happened to Blaine Rising, Marcella Kingman, and James Brayton. However, this trio from the past was soon excited about starting new lives in a futuristic new world. It was filled with amazing technologies and awash with countless new challenges. But soon they discovered a ghastly industry that made robots out of humans. Then to their horror, one in their trio was taken to become a human robot himself.

Join author Don Wilcox as he spins another of his wild science fiction tales, the type of tale that earned him the nickname, "The Mad Man, Don Wilcox."

CAST OF CHARACTERS

BLAINE RISING
It's not easy becoming the leader of a controversial humanitarian insurrection, especially when you're over 150 years old!

J. KARL KARNAIRRE
A shrewd businessman to be sure. He made his fortune in an industry that turned humans into mindless slaves.

MARCELLA KINGMAN RISING
The fate of those she loved depended on her getting very cozy with a man she vehemently detested.

DR. RAVENSTEIN
He knew something had to be done about the legal slave trade around the world. Would he have the strength to do it himself?

JAMES BRAYTON
He was a likable fourteen-year old kid from the distant past, but he kept getting into the worst kind of trouble.

JUDSON
One of Karnairre's men. This stupode manufacturing insider had enough knowledge to bring the entire industry to its knees.

THE ROBOT PERIL

By
DON WILCOX

ARMCHAIR FICTION
PO Box 4369, Medford, Oregon   97501-0168

CHAPTER ONE
The New World

WHEN Blaine Rising came to life in the year 2089, he was amazed by the new world he found. So was his sweetheart, Marcella Kingman; not to mention James Brayton, the fourteen-year-old office boy, who was thrilled to his shoestrings.

All three had emerged from a century and a half of temporary death in a pit of absolute zero, into which they had been hurled by a mad experimenter.

All three had been employed by one of the most extensive and widely renowned science laboratories of the twentieth century. Working together, they had devised a method of preserving living animals for many years in a frozen sleep. But they had never suspected their incredible destiny until the trapdoor leading to the awesome pit had opened beneath their feet. And now, scientists of another era had revived them.

Nineteen hundred and thirty-nine was past and gone. Here was a new life, swifter, more adventurous. At first the pace made them dizzy, but the scientists of this new age were at their side to help them adjust.

In fact, for several weeks the world of science clamored for them. They were conducted over America and Europe, were toasted and interviewed by scientists, historians, reporters. Their tour wound up at Pravianna, one of the great scientific centers of Europe. Pravianna, the cultural and commercial capital of the Central European Confederation.

It was a good place to stop. A gentle old doctor named Ravenstein insisted that his commodious house was to be their home as long as they would stay. For the present, they accepted his hospitality.

He was a most agreeable host. Curiously, he never invited his guests to go through his private laboratories that adjoined his home, nor did anyone else ever enter those sacred recesses. Such privacy was certainly the doctor's privilege. Blaine dismissed it from his mind.

Blaine and his associates were glad to be settled. They needed a springboard from which to plunge into this new life. They were unwilling to be made into museum pieces. Their lives were before them. They must anchor to new purposes.

"We've got to learn fast to catch up," Blaine declared. He and Marcella had been active scientists in the previous century. "Otherwise we'll be three old fogies, in spite of our youth."

"Three Rip Van Winkles without the whiskers," said Jimmie Brayton. He was raring at the bit for adventure. Those silvery futuristic towers of downtown Pravianna tugged at him like a magnet.

Usually there was merriment in Marcella's dark liquid eyes, but Dr. Ravenstein caught signs of hidden apprehension.

"What are you afraid of, Marcella?" he asked her in confidence. His face was kindly, sympathetic.

"Blaine," she answered simply. Then, to the doctor's bewilderment, she explained her fear that there was a hatred buried in Blaine's heart that would have to come out somehow—hatred engendered by the mad experimenter who had certainly deserved execution—and might have gotten it—had he not already been on his death-bed, living in a more horrible suspension of life in poetic justice when Blaine found him. His bones had been dissolved by a strange hormone and he lived on, an incredibly old mass of helpless flesh.

Would the flame of hatred die out, or lurk to blaze up at some unexpected time and place?

The doctor was a keen judge of character and he reassured her. "If Blaine Rising harbors such a hatred, he'll put it to a good use, not a bad one. Pent up feelings give rise to some of the noblest reformers. And besides, fate has already exacted revenge."

BLAINE and Marcella were married. The ceremony was simple, much simpler than the red tape connected with securing a license. To such searching questions as "When did you first contemplate matrimony?" Blaine could only answer, "One hundred and fifty years ago,"—but Dr. Ravenstein was on hand to straighten out all difficulties.

Jimmie Brayton, not wishing to stand in the way of a honeymoon, took the money offered him by Blaine, his chosen guardian, and set out to discover the world for himself. The money had been advanced by a science foundation to give the three a new start in life.

As the lad coasted along on the moving sidewalks through the heart of the glittering, softly humming metropolis, Blaine Rising's words echoed in his ears...

"Don't adventure too long, Jimmie..."

Jimmie's eyes glowed with boyish enthusiasm as he watched his reflections flash along the facades of black glass, while the moving sidewalks carried him in and out of vast buildings. How many boys, he wondered, could resist the temptation to adventure too long if suddenly tossed into this new world of magic?

How many could resist blowing in a pile of money on one of these little red gyroplanes that hopped so nimbly from one roofport to another? Or one of these blue bullet-nosed cars that skimmed so silently over the elevated trafficways? Or one of these protean robots that gleamed through their transparent shells as brilliantly as the insides of a fine watch, and promised to do all your drudgery for a few cents per day?

But Jimmie had no drudgery to do, no highways to follow, no roofports upon which to land. He clung to his money. In time he would need it, no doubt. He saw the wisdom of Blaine's advice. He would not adventure too long. Only a month. Then, according to his promise to Blaine and Marcella, he would return to Dr. Ravenstein's to meet them there.

"One month from today." That was his parting promise, and he and Blaine had shaken hands on it before he struck out.

"Blaine doesn't know me very well yet," thought Jimmie, "but he'll soon learn I'm the kind of guy that never breaks a promise."

The cafeteria door opened for him, a mechanized voice greeted him and asked for his wraps, one mechanical arm took his cap, another presented him with a notched hat check, a voice directed him to the aisle that moved gently past the food counters.

"Watch your step, please," came a mechanized voice, just before he reached the moving aisle. He paused before the electric eye that governed the voice.

"Watch your step, please... Watch your step, please... Watch your step, please..."

He chuckled. More good advice. He'd watch his step all right. He knew the game of self-reliance. He had been an orphan from an early age, had worked hard and played square.

"I'm the kind of guy who never breaks a promise," he repeated to himself as he enjoyed a delicious lunch. Then he pondered. What kind of person would he be in this new world?

He was changed already. Here he sat, wearing these gaudy abbreviated summer clothes—the curious fashion of the times, eating tasty foods that must have been invented for kings, listening to weird sounds that were meant for music, fascinated by dizzying mechanical devices on every hand. Here he sat, trying to peer into this new life that was too dazzling for his mind to penetrate.

One thing he saw clearly, however. In all this fairyland of glittering power, nothing should keep him from *making good* for Blaine Rising. It would take work and study, but he would do it. Blaine and Marcella were determined to find themselves in this new world of science. He would follow in their footsteps and make them proud of him.

"I'll visit factories and mines and laboratories," he vowed to himself, "and when my month is up, I'll start in school where I left off a hundred and fifty years ago, and take up science in earnest…"

AT the close of their month of honeymooning, Mr. and Mrs. Blaine Rising returned to the home of Dr. Ravenstein.

"No, Jimmie hasn't returned yet," said the doctor, "but I've kept in touch with his banker. He cashed only his second travelers' check."

"Where was it cashed?" Blaine asked.

"At Danoba, one of our suburbs, twenty south."

Blaine was satisfied. "He'll be back tonight or tomorrow. I felt sure, when I let him go, that he'd be able to take care of himself."

The doctor was eager to hear Blaine and Marcella's appraisal of the modern world. At dinner he questioned them. Re-examined through their eyes, commonplace things took new significance. The robot, for instance.

"I'm delighted," Blaine declared, "to see how important the robot has become. We found them at work in vast numbers."

"Robot Manufacturing is our fastest growing industry."

"In my day we were never optimistic about the robot's prospects," Blaine confessed. "I thought it would never be more than a glorified mechanical toy for the amusement of a few people. But a century and a half makes a great difference."

Dr. Ravenstein glowed, for he was proud of his own robot and he loved to describe its many uses. "It's an eighty-seven model—not strictly up-to-date, but good enough for our purposes. I don't believe in trading them in every year, as some do."

At the touch of a button the robot rolled into the room. It was an obelisk of noiseless power, as tall as a man, riding on silent rubber wheels.

Marcella and Blaine had seen it before, and hundreds of others like it, so they showed no surprise as it extended a collapsible shelf for their plates. This was customary. A moment later it returned laden with the desserts, then wheeled back into the other room.

"But I thought robots would look like men," Marcella protested.

"Marcella is quite disappointed," her husband explained with a laugh, "because they don't have a closer resemblance to human beings."

"Some resemblance is inevitable, but many early models strove for more than was practical," Ravenstein explained. "Their modern form has been determined largely by their functions. It is their efficient service, not their romantic appearance, that makes them sell by the millions."

Blaine saw the point. "Wheels are better than feet, for most locomotion."

"Right," said the doctor, "but of course they also have suction feet to use when needed. They're a marvelous composite of machines—easy to set for a new task—and their combinations are almost unlimited. Man has only two hands; the robot has many."

"Then I presume," said Blaine casually, "that no one could persuade you to exchange your robot for a stupode?"

DR. RAVENSTEIN colored. Why this remark should cause an intense feeling to rise within him was more than his guests could understand. After a moment of awkward pause he said, "So you've bumped into stupodes."

"Yes," said Blaine, puzzled by the doctor's strange manner. "We bumped into them—"

"Literally, in fact," said Marcella, "or rather, they bumped into us. It was in the station as we started on our tour. We had never seen any before."

"Personally, I don't care if I never see another," said Blaine crisply. The doctor's silence on this topic was again noticeable. Was it possible, Blaine wondered, that this kindly old doctor had something to do with the strange dehumanized forms called stupodes?

Another embarrassing silence, but Marcella came to the rescue. "In fact, we had never heard of them. We're still curious to know what brand of bird, beast, or fish they are."

"What did they look like?" the doctor asked, as if to probe their feelings further.

"Like any other human beings," said Marcella; "but they wore crazy black and white stiff collars and very dumb expressions."

"There were three of them with this party of travelers," Blaine explained, "and all three wore high checkered collars. Otherwise there was nothing distinctive about their clothing. They seemed to be porters. They marched along, loaded down with luggage, followed by some wealthy-looking gentlemen who strutted like so many oriental potentates. I didn't care for their airs. We stepped to one side to view the procession, but one of these checkered collars strode right into us with no more manners than a blind horse. No excuse for it, and I told him so."

"You doubled your fists," said Marcella excitedly.

"I admit I had a rash impulse to hit him when he didn't even turn to apologize, but one of the aristocrats shouted, 'Don't strike him! He's only a stupode...' That was the first we knew of them."

The doctor nodded noncommittally. "You have to make allowances for stupodes. They're not responsible; they simply follow directions."

"We saw others from time to time," Marcella added, "and they all had a very unintelligent look. The checkered collar is evidently a standard identification."

"The very sight of them is highly repulsive," said Blaine, while his wife nodded her agreement, at the same time wondering if their outspoken opinions offended their host.

"The Stupodes Corporation has put them on the market quite recently, and it is perhaps too early to say whether they will be a success," said Ravenstein dryly, "but if you find them repulsive to the sight, that may be because you aren't adjusted to some of our ways in this new century."

"I'll never adjust to a return of slavery. I thought we were past the age of traffic in human flesh and blood." Blaine saw no reason to pull his punches.

"Correction," said the doctor, whose manner grew increasingly reserved. "Stupodes are not legally human."

"Not *legally human*? What do you mean?" Blaine asked.

"The standards for being human have raised in the past century. The Central European Confederation has seen to that. Since the Uplift Act of a few years ago, a segment of the population has been removed to an Uplift Colony in Africa. They were the mentally unfortunate—usually with glandular deficiencies—creatures who were found to lack the intelligence or other requirements necessary to be human beings, as defined by the act of the Confederation. Now the Uplift Colony supplies raw material to the Stupodes Corporation, whose plant is also in Africa."

Blaine sighed with indignation until his wife clutched his arm and reminded him of his manners.

"The democratic ideal was strong with us," she apologized, "so you'll have to forgive us if we can't appreciate—"

"But it's not only the democratic ideal," Blaine continued, "it's the responsibility of science—medicine—eugenics. Why, in Heaven's name, should there be any persons without full capacities for intelligence and—"

He stopped short. Ravenstein eyed him so intently that he came down to earth with a thud. After all, he was not aware of all the ropes of the new century. He was in no position to slur the progress of medicine or insult this gentle doctor who was his host.

"Your perspective is unique, I grant," the doctor said in a cool, even tone. "Just what did you expect of medical science?"

"I didn't expect it to betray unfortunates who are born with low mental capacities or other tendencies to become inferior. Even in my day—" Blaine caught himself glorying in the promise of science of the earlier century, "medicine had made a great start through the study of glands and the chemical synthesis of hormones."

"Yes," his wife chimed in. "In our own laboratories we learned to reverse the 'peck order' in a flock of hens—you know, treating the last hen, that all the others pecked, so that it became first and could peck all the others."

The doctor smiled at the mention of this familiar classic. "The stupode is, quite literally speaking, a human robot, and the Stupodes Corporation means to keep him that way, not change him. The medical advances have been employed to standardize his dull wits so that he bends readily to his master's needs."

"It's an outrage," Blaine blazed. "Human robots? It's a prostitution of science…"

"You are welcome to your own opinion; however, before you declare war on the stupode industry, or even declare your opinions too dogmatically, perhaps you should know your grounds more thoroughly. I propose that we have a salesman drop in some evening this week and demonstrate the wares of the Stupodes Corporation. Perhaps we shall change our minds."

"Very well," said Blaine, but in his heart he knew he would never condone human slavery, even though whitewashed by the name of science.

CHAPTER TWO
Lost, Strayed, or Stolen—Jimmie

THE stupode salesman was engaged to come two days hence. The Risings waited eagerly. In the meantime their troubles thickened.

In the first place, Jimmie Brayton did not return. Marcella grew worried. Her husband had agreed to be legally responsible for the lad. Was he stuck with a fickle child who would prove a burden?

Blaine did not think so. He liked the boy too much to believe he had gotten into trouble. Doubtless it was simply the novelty of things—the freedom, money, adventure. Enough to make any boy forget to come home. Give him time.

Had Blaine known the contents of a letter Dr. Ravenstein carried, his complacency over Jimmie would have shattered. But the doctor absent-mindedly forgot the letter. Blaine became preoccupied with the stupode movement.

A reformer's zeal suddenly rose within him. It hurt him to see civilized people drift into such a deplorable practice. The more he read of the industry, the more he yearned to fight against it. Marcella shared his indignation.

In their eyes it was a treacherous menace, spreading like slow poison through the lifeblood of the nation. Had it been fire or a disease or a visible disintegration of buildings and crops, the people would have howled for deliverance! But it was far more insidious than any such spectacular destruction. Stealthily it gnawed at the fibers of democratic society, made pitiful victims of the very people science could help most, planted the seeds of an evil caste system.

"We've got to fight it," Blaine declared over and over again.

"Then we'd better break off from Dr. Ravenstein at once," Marcella concluded. "Our decision may embarrass him. There's something mysterious about his connections with stupodes. He knows how we feel, but still he never says a word. I'm afraid we've spoken out of turn. If we expect to fight the stupode movement, we'd better learn all we can about it and hold our tongues."

ON the evening of the demonstration, the Risings were ready. They would play the game of prospective buyers, pretend approval, and hide their bitter feelings.

The doorbell rang.

"That must be Mr. Falliman coming to show us a stupode," said the doctor, setting his coffee aside. "I'll have the robot show him in." His hands skipped over the portable keyboard—a sort of miniature typewriter in appearance—to direct the marvelous machine by remote control.

The robot rolled through the front hallway to open the door, greet the guest and his stupode in Dr. Ravenstein's own voice, dispose of their wraps, and show them into the reception room. Soon Marcella, Blaine, and the doctor joined them.

A few words of acquaintance and the sharp-tongued little salesman plunged into his well-practiced demonstration speech.

"This fellow's name is George."

His audience studied the stupode in wonderment, while that sluggish creature stared, dull-eyed, at nothing in particular.

"He is typical of thousands we have ready for the market," said the sleek little Mr. Falliman. "No intelligence, no sentiments, no curiosity, no sex appeal."

George remained expressionless. His head leaned slightly to one side, rested upon the stiff black and white checkered collar that clasped his neck. He was a big fellow and Falliman enjoyed demonstrating his strength.

Dr. Ravenstein stood well to one side. The good humor was gone from his face, now flushed with unspoken feeling. He breathed heavily as he witnessed the spectacle of a helpless stupode being put through demonstrations.

"He never wears out," Falliman boasted. "Even if he did, he'd keep on working. He doesn't have the nerve to disobey." He slapped the stupode across the cheek to prove his point. "See? No feelings. I've lashed George with a horsewhip, and he didn't mind. Did you, George?" Falliman sneered cynically.

A weak smile registered on the timid face. George winced a little and uttered an answer in slow, plaintive words. "I minded a little—but—" He could get no farther.

"But you couldn't help yourself," Falliman cut in. The stupode nodded and blushed. His demonstrator carried on proudly. "There's the answer to the world's labor problems. You can't excel a stupode for cheap, efficient industry—and no back talk! Teach him a hand skill, give him a place to sleep and eat, lock a checkered collar around his neck so he won't get mixed up with normal human beings, and there you've got it. The solution to human drudgery in a nutshell. Mechanical robots can't compare—"

"Are you selling lots of them?" Blaine asked.

"Confidentially," Falliman said, "this is the fastest growing industry on the continent. And of course it's only in its infancy. We're trying to hold back to avoid arousing any unfavorable public sentiment. We choose our clients with care. But we've already sold to a few of the richest and most prominent persons in the country. I venture to say that within two years..." The spokesman concluded with a sweeping gesture; his prospects were too great for words.

"I presume they have a great many uses," Marcella ventured.

"Unlimited," said the salesman, and he loosed another volley of oratory. "A most important angle. They are available not only for general manual labor and monotonous factory jobs, but also for a host of specialized needs." He gave numerous illustrations, explaining that various glandular treatments gave them certain desired characteristics.

"For example, we have a special class of stupode that we call the cringer. Now, George, here, is not a cringer, are you, George?"

The big childish face twitched slightly as Falliman yanked at the hair and slapped the cheeks. Blaine, standing close beside Marcella, felt her shudder.

"But we could make a cringer out of George if the purchaser preferred," said the stupode salesman blithely. "It's all a matter of taste, you know. Some people like to see their subordinates wince, and some don't. Or we could make a weeper out of him, though we don't often have calls for weepers. However, one of the most exclusive mortuaries in this city purchased a number of weepers, and they are giving splendid satisfaction. They don't wear the regulation collar while on duty, of course. They are trained to mix with the mourners and friends to lend perfect atmosphere. But, speaking of the regulation collar—get down on your knees, George, and let's take a look at your collar."

The big, helpless creature obeyed.

"This trick serves as a protection for both humans and stupodes. It's an identification the owner can put on or take off at will; but the stupode can't remove it."

"Why not?"

"It's too complicated. It requires five motions to unlock. His mentality doesn't reach that far."

"But his manual skills—" Blaine protested.

"The wise owner never teaches him how to work it." The demonstration went on over the back of George's neck. One simple motion to lock, five to unlock. Blaine practiced, and the motions quickly became automatic for his skillful fingers. The others practiced, too, while Falliman talked on. He told the history of the development. The government had given the Stupodes Corporation a special franchise, with exclusive rights to the growing population of the Uplift Colony. Perfect raw material. The corporation's scientists were privileged to grade and sort and treat these creatures that had been adjudged non-human under the Uplift Act of '65.

FALLIMAN turned to the doctor. "Being a physician, you no doubt remember that the Uplift Administration combed the country for qualified scientists to carry on the movement."

Ravenstein's lips drew down. There was a sharp clash of eyes between him and the salesman, who rambled on.

"A great thing for the human race. Onward and upward to higher standards. A continual purification. The schools keep the program moving. They cull out the dullards and the freaks, and send them down to the Uplift Colony. In fact, the colony was getting crowded until the Stupodes Corporation thinned them out. It was the human thing to do. That patch of territory down on the African coast is pretty dreary, even for non-humans. It's better to convert them into domestic animals and put them to use. And what a demand—already our business is world wide."

"I think it's wonderful..." Marcella managed a convincing tone.

"This is all new to us," said Blaine, "because we've been out of touch with American life for some time. But we are professional scientists ourselves. We want to learn more about this movement—perhaps have a share in its destiny."

The enthusiastic Falliman was sure he could help them make the right contacts. They must attend the forthcoming National Stupodes Show, to be held in the city. He could arrange reservations for them. The great Karnairre himself, president of the Stupodes Corporation, would be there. Perhaps they could meet him—

Falliman left with no sale but with a full head of enthusiasm. George had performed perfectly. His good manners were at last automatic. He would not have to be horsewhipped tonight.

As their footsteps echoed away, the little group in the reception room sat and stared in silent rage. Blaine was a bombshell of indignation. But it was the doctor who exploded.

"I can see you haven't changed your minds," he said, looking from one to the other. "You hate this stupode industry as bitterly as ever."

The Risings studied their host's fiery eyes. They had not seen this round, baldish, good-natured doctor show his fighting face until this moment. They nodded and held their tongues.

"All right. Let me tell you something." The doctor was on the edge of his seat. "Blaine Rising, from the instant you first spoke of stupodes, I knew you were the man I've been looking for—to lead the movement against this human curse..."

Marcella gasped. The white widened in Blaine's eyes.

"I didn't state my position before," Ravenstein continued, "for I didn't want my prejudices to influence you. But I've been proud every minute for the staunch stand you've both taken." He shook them by the hands. "I've tried to fight this thing," he went on, "but I'm too old, and leadership needs the magnetism of youth. But you've got everything, Blaine…energy and courage and idealism—and a talented wife to help you. The medical world is already interested in you because of your sensational return to life."

Visions rose in Blaine's mind as the doctor continued his spirited rhapsody. "I've fought a losing game, Blaine, but you may win where I've failed. You won't be alone. There are thousands of individual doctors over the country who, even though despondent, are ready to join the fight. They know— as you and I know—that stupodes could be made into normal men."

"Then why—"

"Because we're hamstrung—shackled by laws—forbidden to use hormone treatments on human patients without a special license—and who gets a license? Only those few doctors who sell their souls to a political party—the Uplifters—who swept into the capital on a wave of fanaticism. For the last quarter of a century the Uplifters have played steamroller politics. They've saddled laws on the Confederation that no self-respecting doctor or eugenicist or educator could condone!"

"But the doctors who sell their souls for licenses?"

"They carry on their outrageous experiments in the privacy of the African laboratories—on handsome salaries. There you have it—politics at its worst—the nation too comfortable in its modern mechanical luxuries to be bothered—and the unfortunate tenth of the population due to be dressed down as stupodes and whipped into slavery…"

BLAINE paced the floor. The doctor's fighting face cooled. He watched the young man before him eagerly. Here was decision in the making. With swift action this menace might be nipped in the bud, though the steamroller gained momentum every hour.

"But why should the Uplifters want these things?" Marcella asked. "Why, with such wonderful robots to do man's work, why do they need stupodes? Do they really think they are raising the standards for being human?"

"Bosh!" roared the doctor. "It's nothing but highly organized snobbery. There are always some people who can't enjoy life unless they are trampling some of their fellow humans in the dust. Here…" The doctor drew some papers from his inner coat pocket. "…look at some typical Uplifter propaganda."

He spread the papers on the table, and Marcella caught the title, "The Social Distinction of Owning Stupodes."

"Oh, by George!" the doctor suddenly shouted, picking up an envelope from among the pamphlets. "Here's something I forgot. Come here, Blaine."

The envelope contained a note from the banker concerning Jimmie Brayton's travelers' checks. There were the notations copied from each check, which the banker thought might be helpful in tracing the missing boy. Blaine and the others poured over the information.

The first check was cashed here in the city, "For instruction in operating robots, and cash."

The second, given at Danoba, a suburb: "For enrollment fee, Danoba Technical School, and cash."

The third, of recent date, was simply marked, "For Cash." It was given at Uplift Harbor, Africa.

"Africa—!" Marcella gave a startled cry. Fear struck home within her.

Blaine broke for the telephones, dialed one, gave the receiver to the robot, dialed another, tapped off the seconds with tense fingers. Marcella looked on through frightened eyes, while the doctor sank to a chair and clutched his head, mumbling apologies for forgetting he had the letter.

"Don't worry," said Blaine. "I'll get to the bottom of it. The boy may simply be adventuring, but he's worth better care than I've given him—Marcella, if I have to make a trip, I want you and Dr. Ravenstein to attend the National Stupodes Show—get all the information you can—make contact with those in charge. We've got a fight on our hands—as soon as we find Jimmie…"

"Blaine, dear, you'll be careful, won't you—"

Long distance from Africa came on the line. Swift service this hour of the night. Blaine put his questions sharply. There was an anxious moment of waiting. Then—

"I'm sorry, but we do not know of a Jimmie Brayton. If he has been here, we have no record…"

Failing to get any lead, Blaine reluctantly hung up. Another call sounded through the robot's speaker—the African Laboratories of the Stupodes Corporation. Blaine pleaded for information but got none. The Corporation would reveal no names, answer no complaints, make no special investigations, accept no visitors. Blaine hung up in a subdued rage.

He tried to reach the president of the corporation, who was thought to be in his Pravianna office, but without success. The great Karnairre could not be found at this hour of the night. The next best bet was a crisply delivered night letter, which would overtake him by tomorrow.

In the meantime Marcella dialed a suburban number, and Blaine took the phone.

"Yes, Jimmie Brayton enrolled with us," said a secretary at the Danoba Technical School. "He was very anxious to get started in science—"

"Where is he now?"

"Unfortunately he had no credentials, and his story was most fantastic…"

"But where is he?"

"You'll have to call someone on the examinations staff—"

The examinations official came back with icy but informative answers. "You are aware, Mr. Rising, that the Uplift Act requires that certain intelligence and achievement tests be given a student enrolling in a new school. Brayton proved to be deficient in mentality. He excelled in only one field—the ability to operate a robot. Beyond that he demonstrated vast ignorance. He was confused about his own age, and he couldn't even name the last three Confederation presidents. Our school is no place for him. We had no legal alternative but to turn him over to the Uplift Court. I'm sorry, we cannot make any exceptions…"

At last the telephone operators found the judge of the local Uplift Court, whose stony words turned terrified suspicions into cold, hard fact. Blaine slammed the telephone down, white with anger.

"Help me pack, quick. I'm flying to Africa at once. They've got Jimmie…"

CHAPTER THREE
Stupodes in the Making

J. KARL KARNAIRRE loved importance almost as much as wealth. He never strode into the offices of the Stupodes Corporation unaware of the rich bonanza that lay before him. His, by the virtue of swift wits, smooth manners, and a shrewd tie-up with the inner ring of Uplifters. His, by virtue of *grasp*.

With business booming, a national show for this city just a few days ahead, and a favorable editorial on stupodes in the morning paper, the great Karnairre reminded himself that he was Central Europe's man of the hour. Here in Pravianna he maintained his sanctum sanctorum, keeping his finger on the public pulse, and directing the African Laboratories by remote control.

His secretaries, alert with respect for his domineering personality, gathered about him with their day's problems. They waited in silence while he settled his huge body back of the silvered ebony desk. Then, from the flash of his dark eyes and the haughty thrust of his trim black beard, they knew he was ready to shoot decisions right and left.

"Who's first? Blittstein?"

"Mr. Karnairre, our African office reports that our increased sales will shrink our reserves within a year, unless we can bring the raw material in faster."

"I'm working on that," the huge man snapped in his brittle voice. "I've got the Confederation hatching a law to cut deeper into the civilian population as well as the schools. Tell the laboratories that. They can put the present raw material into stupode collars as fast as possible. We won't run out. Next…"

"Mr. Karnairre—"

"Speak up…speak up…"

"The Uplift Colony tells us they are besieged with inquiries on cases for whom they have no records. They suggest it might be better if they had a chance to at least register their new inmates before we shunt them to our laboratories."

"No." the president said firmly with a jump of his pointed black beard. "Needless waste of time. The fewer records, the better. It's the easiest way to kill complaints. Next…"

"Mr. Karnairre, the salesmen are still continually faced with the same question from customers: Shouldn't the stupodes be de-sexed?"

"The answer is still no. Our pituitary treatments retire all social impulses. We've yet to have a single case of social misbehavior. Tell your customers that. Further operations are unnecessary. But remember, if you ever find an exception to our clean record, report it at once. Next…"

"The salesmen also have occasional calls for female stupodes—"

"Tell the customers not this season. Perhaps later. But don't tell them why. The facts are, we must wait for public sentiment to mellow; furthermore, at the rate we're expanding, we may soon need the best women inmates of the Uplift Colony to provide us with regular new raw material. Next…"

"I'm sorry to bring it up again, Mr. Karnairre—"

"Out with it, Judson."

"I have some very urgent inquiries about cases we've taken. From relatives and friends who demand—"

"Demand, nothing," Karnairre nearly scowled. "We never answer complaints—*never.*"

"But here's one from a prominent scientist, Blai—"

"*No!*" Karnairre's great fist slammed the table. "We never tell anybody anything. The law's behind us. That's good enough. Why get into personal tangles? If you weaken once more on that point, Judson, I'll wrap a stupode collar around your own neck. Any more business?"

A FEW thousand miles to the south Jimmie Brayton leaned with his back against a wall of natural rock. A chill breeze swept along the foot of the coastal mountains—it was winter farther south—but the rock ledge was warm and the tropical sun was generous.

Jimmie was hungry. None of the eight or nine thousand creatures imprisoned in this pen could be any hungrier than he was. His eyes burned. He was almost too sick to keep on guard. But he was still Jimmie Brayton, not a stupode. They hadn't caught him yet.

Hunger and burning eyes were the price he paid to keep from being overtaken by the officials who moved through the pen to fell the daily harvest—officials popularly known as Knockouts. The dreaded Knockouts carried deadly hypodermic needles. When they slipped up behind you and pierced you with their needles, you dropped off to sleep in your tracks. Later, you woke up in a laboratory, but before you left you were no longer human.

You were a stupode.

The Knockouts might have got Jimmie five minutes after he first arrived, if it hadn't been for Tony. Tony had been here for many months and knew the ropes. He knew the Knockouts followed no system in selecting their victims, and that was worth knowing from the start. Tony was a pal.

The Knockouts simply plowed through the sluggish crowd wherever it was thickest and injected the potent serum indiscriminately. Then a corps of trained stupodes would follow through with stretchers to pick up the ones that dropped, then cart them off to the laboratories.

A large majority of these men and boys were pitiful, simple creatures. They had no conception of hovering danger. But there were all grades, and many freaks that fell into no class whatever.

A few, like Jimmie and Tony, were sensitive to every move of the Knockouts. They knew that eternal vigilance was the price of avoiding stupode-hood. The vigilant ones planned together, devised warning signals, stood guard for each other while they slept. They passed their nights in the outdoors near the perpendicular wall of rock, avoiding the ghastly sleeping halls where danger always lurked.

However, the Knockouts occasionally changed their tactics. That was how they finally got Tony. They waited just inside the doors of the dining halls and touched their needles to the incoming procession. A few days after that began, the vigilant gang quickly became depleted. Some were caught, a few went mad from worry, so Jimmie decided to go it alone.

HE tried to keep his wits sharp, but now hunger and fatigue dragged him down. All his fanciful schemes to beat this game wore down to vague animal cravings.

A sweet mess! And to think he'd come out of a century and a half of ice, only to be snatched up for this. It was nauseating. Yet in all this agony nothing stung deeper than the inner feeling that he had failed Blaine and Marcella.

He wished now he'd bought a robot instead of enrolling in school. The tons of fun he could have had! The one he learned on was a nifty. It had everything. Press here, and it reached. Press here, and it turned on the voice records that were hidden within it; or press there, and it took a talking movie of everything before it. And all at the same time it would roll along, or jump, or cling, or lift and deposit—the recombinations were unlimited. Jimmie would never forget how he amazed his instructor when he discovered how to make his robot tie a four-in-hand tie. There was an art to working those keyboards, and he'd just begun to find it.

If he only had one of those mechanical men here! How it would tear through the barbed wire fence or clamber over the smooth-hewn stone embankment.

"H-s-s-st!"

Jimmie cocked his ears, scanned his surroundings for Knockouts before looking up. He knew that hissing sound. Joe, the beggar. His tousled head peeked over the crest of the ledge.

"Brought you somethin'," he called in a low voice. A paper sack dropped down into the pen. Jimmie caught it, dived into it, ate like a starved dog.

"You're a pal, Joe," he gasped between bites. The money he'd passed through the fence from time to time had proved a lucky investment over and over. This heap of rags was no common chiseler. He claimed to have been a guide at one time in the desolate regions before the Confederation mapped the land for a colony. He was starved for companionship and Jimmie had won him over, heart and soul.

"You take too many chances," the boy called up to him. "The guards will get suspicious and toss you in, and the Knockouts will get us both."

He craned his neck to see whether his warning registered. Joe sat like a bronze statue. His clothes were good camouflage against the brown surface rock. At that moment another brown face appeared over the ledge—the long, comical face of a pack mule.

Jimmie gulped. "What in the sam hill…?"

"But you wish to escape."

"Of course, but—"

"Then come on. All is ready. I have Chumpo loaded with food."

Jimmie blinked, turned his wistful eyes toward the formidable barrier of mountains and back to the comical face of Chumpo. A magic carpet couldn't have jolted him any more suddenly. He realized that to escape the way he had come was out of the question. He would never get beyond Uplift Harbor, and then back he would come in handcuffs to his eventual fate. But the mountains—and this curious old beggar—it seemed like a dream.

Or was it the answer to a dream? Somewhere beyond those tortuous trails lay the Plegungdo and Traable Railway that led to Debenz, an airport.

"Joe!" he whispered excitedly. "Do you mean it? Do you think we could do it?"

A rope slithered down the wall. Jimmie's eyes cast about in terror. "Careful, Joe. If a Knockout sees us—"

"They won't," Joe grumbled. "They're all watchin' the fracas over by the gate. I came by a couple minutes ago. Some stranger was tryin' to argue his way in, to look for someone, and he was right handy with his fists. I see they're still going it," his keen eyes glinted into the distance, "so now's time for a get-away."

Jimmie would have preferred darkness, but he recalled the searching spotlight that combed the grounds by night. He looked far across the pen, saw that a first rate commotion was in progress outside the gate. A huddle of guards struggled to control a berserk figure without success. Joe was right; the Knockouts wouldn't miss a spectacle like that. There would never be a better moment to escape. With these lightning thoughts, Jimmie seized the rope and bounded up the wall.

"Darned lucky if we get away with this!" he panted. They scouted over a knoll and dragged Chumpo after them. One parting backward glance told them the fighting stranger had won his point, for they saw him leap over the gate into the pen. Joe pointed and said, "I think he had a gun."

Only when the prison was many miles back of them did Jimmie's nerves quiet down enough to let him be curious about the incident.

"Wonder who the stranger was, and who do you suppose he was after?"

Joe shook his head. "No difference. The Knockouts were waiting. His ill fate...your good fortune."

CHAPTER FOUR
Checkered Collar Parade

THE National Stupodes Show.

The greatest display of stupodes the world had ever seen. Stupodes of all grades and specialties on demonstration in their respective booths. Stupodes doing all kinds of drudgery—feeding machines, heaving bricks, pasting labels, swinging mauls.

A colossal show in the arena afternoon and night with checkered collars by the hundreds. Through the vast auditorium bands blared, crowds cheered, colored lights flashed in splendor. Training demonstrations, stunts of dumb strength, exhibitions of obedience and cringing and weeping and taking punishment, endurance treadmills until the poor creatures collapsed from exhaustion—such was the glorious spectacle provided by the great Karnairre.

"STUPODES FOR SALE ON THE PREMISES."

The sign flashed gayly over the entrance to the merchandise rooms. There sat rows of collared creatures, placarded and tagged. Laborers already skilled in this or that; house servants with minds too weak to remember conversations and bear tales; audience packers and political rally specialists trained to look attentive and applaud upon signal; stunts men ready to run through flames or leap from towers in blind obedience to commands.

And how they sold! Toward the final days of the show Karnairre sent a rush order to the African Laboratories for more merchandise.

It was no wonder he gloated. Public sentiment continued to bend in his direction, an obeisance to his canny genius.

The yapping of his enemies was drowned out by the clink of inpouring shekels.

No need to worry about the case that was scheduled go to the Superior Court a few weeks hence. Most of the judges saw straight on these matters. And there was plenty of "insurmountable" proof that stupodes weren't really human, by modern standards anyway. The Court would put its okay on that, and stupode commerce would roll on without a wobble. And there would be a lot of free publicity.

Yes, Karnairre told himself, unquestionably he was the nation's man of the hour. He could order life to his own taste—and he did! Champagne parties every night. New females to tease his fancy with their laughter and beauty.

And by the way, that was a lovely new number he'd added to his guest list for tonight. A bit shy, but desperately beautiful. Champagne and laughter and his own ready bawdy wit would break down that cool reserve. What was her name? Oh, yes—Rising—Mrs. Rising. He *should* remember, for she had frequently attended the daily receptions, following the afternoon shows in which he and his officers presented themselves to the public.

The three airliner loads of new stupodes trudged into the arena. The huge black-bearded industrial magnate capered through his inspections, fairly floating on inflated importance.

"They're perfect," he exulted. "Perfect! Go ahead and put them into the afternoon show. Don't forget to send me a dozen of the handsomest for my roof party tonight. My guests like to buy them for souvenirs. That's all. I'm off for the day."

THAT afternoon Marcella and Dr. Ravenstein sat in their usual places down close to the great arena.

Watching the show had been dreary business for them from the first. Now it was sheer mockery. They were desperate for news of Blaine and Jimmie.

Blaine hadn't communicated since his second day in Africa. At that time he had fought his way into the offices and demanded information on Jimmie. There was no record of the boy. But Blaine—sure he was on the trail—had finally received a half-hearted permission to comb the place. He had promised to call as soon as there was any news. In the meantime they must carry on as planned.

All that was weeks ago. Now Dr. Ravenstein held a tight grip on himself to keep from telling Marcella his terrible fears. She was a courageous thing, so fearless she would have gone in pursuit of Blaine days ago had the doctor not dissuaded her.

"He'll be back, don't you worry. He's probably collecting some valuable information and doesn't dare call for fear of being suspected—"

"But he could write…"

"Yes, of course," the doctor admitted, "that is, if he isn't too busy. Yes, he really ought to write—" The doctor looked into her eyes looking for a sign of hope, but what was the use. His arguments were worn out and the girl knew it. Something terrible had happened; there was no sense in trying to kid themselves out of it. Many wives would have suffered an emotional breakdown. Marcella held on with steel nerves.

She pinned all her hopes on one strategy—a direct appeal to the great Karnairre. If that failed…

But it must not!

Tonight she would face him, win his friendship, and implore his help.

"If you're determined to keep that engagement tonight, I'm going with you," the doctor declared.

"Thank you," the girl said softly.

Then an announcement blared from the loud speakers. Silence fell over the audience as they listened.

"Now entering the arena from the south end—a company of brand new stupodes, 2090 models—(applause)—just arrived from the African Laboratories—for your approval. (Applause.) They embody all the latest achievements in stupode cultures. They will now parade through the arena for their first public inspection. (Applause.) Lieutenant Braba, winner of three medals for the training of cringers, wields the whip." (Applause.)

And the whip cracked.

The procession trailed into sight trudging single file. An endless line of colorful uniforms, black and white checkered collars, expressionless faces. Somewhere a military band cut loose with a lively number.

Around the arena the stupodes moved. Now and then the lash fell on a laggard, who would yelp pitifully and jump back into time.

The drummer in the band, with a flare for the dramatic, watched for Braba's whip to descend, so he could smash out a cymbal crash in time with a stupode's jump. He achieved a comic effect with every crash. The amused thousands responded with ripples of mirth and applause.

But comedy and tragedy are often close together.

A minute after the drummer's fun reached its height, a strange tragic atmosphere descended upon the scene.

IT began inconspicuously. A few spectators noticed that a lovely girl, who sat beside a baldish, professional-looking old man, suddenly rose to her feet. Her dark liquid eyes were intent upon a certain part of the parade, as if fixed upon one stupode. The rather large handsome creature parading directly before her seemed to be the target of her fascination.

Her terror-struck manner shocked the crowds close about her. The elderly man clutched at her hand and gasped, "Marcella...what's the matter...?"

The girl did not hear. She was not aware of the presence of anyone—human or stupode—except that one creature, a handsome specimen with a pale, expressionless face.

"Blaine!" she cried out.

In a trance of terror, she ran down to the arena wall, calling. The stupodes plodded on, single file, oblivious to their surroundings. The line filled half a circumference of the arena. Marcella moved with it, her eyes intent upon one form. She found her way out onto the broad floor, moved by fits and starts, cried out, though her words would not carry against the thumping band music.

The elderly man came after her and tried to call her back. Sections of the vast audience came to their feet, struck by this unaccountable drama. Throughout the auditorium people pointed, whispered, and craned to see. The confusion grew stronger, the band music faded. Curiosity spread over the thousands like an electric wind. The band director, waving furiously to keep the music going, turned and saw what the others saw. His hand froze, poised in mid-air. The music broke off.

All eyes were upon the girl, her extended arms and fingers that seemed to implore as she followed after the certain stupode. The amazed spectators could not mistake the meaning; it was the terrified recognition of a loved one turned stupode...

Over the soft tread of feet, over echoed whispers, the girl's cry sounded.

"Blaine! *Blaine!* It's me, Blaine, Marcella...your wife! Look at me, darling. Tell me you know me, Blaine...Blaine! Heavens...what have they done to you?"

The confusion of the crowd grew loud enough to drown out Marcella's voice as excited people rose from their seats in sympathetic alarm. Then came a wave of perfect silence, as if the very auditorium missed a heartbeat and held its breath. The girl caught the arm of the handsome, pitiful creature. He hesitated at her touch, then turned with expressionless eyes.

Thousands too far away to catch the words listened to the echoes of the pleading voice and were paralyzed by its tragic emotion.

"Blaine...it's me...Marcella. Don't you know me?"

The gap in the marching line widened before them, while back of them the oncoming stupodes gathered closer.

Whispers sifted through the audience.

"Look...he seems to recognize—"

Hushed whispers followed. The whispers of hearts throbbing in sadness to stark human tragedy, of minds magnetized in mass pity.

In that tense moment the brilliantly uniformed Lieutenant Braba flourished his whip and strode to the break in the parade line. The whip lashed out...

Whizz—crack!

Wincing creatures uttered cries and marched on in dumb obedience. But one figure caught by the lash went down with the shock of pain—the figure of Marcella. Her stifled cry of pain echoed through the building.

At that instant literally thousands of boos were heard. Dozens of persons near the scene rushed down into the arena toward the pain-stricken girl.

Dr. Ravenstein, already trudging as fast as his aging figure would go, was first there. He gathered the fainting form into his arms and bore her off through an arena exit.

It was several minutes before the boos of the audience quieted. Not until the flashy lieutenant conducted his company off the floor did the jeering begin to subside. Then the people sat again, dazed, stunned, silently reflective. The show carried on, under the blare of trumpets and the crash of cymbals, but the spirit was gone out of it.

CHAPTER FIVE
Jimmie Returns

THE doctor and several volunteer assistants rushed the agonized girl into a hospital car. The doors closed. The high-powered vehicle rolled up onto the trafficway. A cooling breeze poured through. The girl's eyes opened a little; her white lips trembled.

The doctor watched intently and administered every care. He was scarcely aware that another person sat in the corner of the ambulance, looking on with deep sympathy. He spoke to the girl in a soft voice and advised her to close her eyes and rest. Cool applications to her face made her breathe more easily.

"Where are we going?" she asked.

"Wherever you wish—home if you like—or the hospital," he said gently, soothingly.

"Let's just ride awhile," she suggested weakly. "It seems restful and I'm sure it will help a lot."

The doctor smiled at her and conveyed her wish to the driver. As they spun along she tried to relax, but it was not easy. Thoughts tormented her.

"I'm sorry I acted so—so—"

"But you didn't," the doctor said quickly. "Many a mind would have snapped under such a shock. You're all right, Marcella."

"No, I lost my grip on myself. Somehow it struck me as more shocking than even death. I still can't realize—" She shuddered and closed her eyes painfully. "I should have guessed—" Her dark eyes filled with tears and her head turned away.

There was a long silence as the venerable man watched over her weeping form. The car rolled on noiselessly. Inwardly Ravenstein blamed himself. Why had he been so ineffectual in the face of this fearsome peril? Why hadn't he foreseen the worst and prepared her with a hint? Instead he had denied that the worst could come. After all of his professional years he was still a victim of that treacherous human weakness—optimism. Bitter thoughts.

Once he glanced toward the semi-dark corner of the ambulance but did not recognize the bronzed face that looked on so silently, and he was too much preoccupied with his own remorse to be curious.

Gradually Marcella's manner changed. The medicine restored her energy. She reached for her handkerchief, brushed away her tearstains, rose up on one elbow, and let her eyes rove over the passing scenery. She gave a passing glance to the silent occupant whose face was lost in shadows, then turned to Dr. Ravenstein with determination.

"I must get home," she said. "I have an engagement with Karnairre tonight. I'm going to demand my husband."

The doctor smiled and shook his head decisively. "You must rest tonight. Forget everything and rest, for your own good. You can't defy such a shock as this."

"Take me home," Marcella demanded. "I'm going to keep my engagement. Karnairre doesn't know who I am, but he likes me. It's my big chance. I'll win his confidence, then make him give me back Blaine as they took him from me." The girl's eyes lit up with violence. "If he won't do it, I'll—"

Ravenstein put his fingers to her lips to stop her rash speech, then he glanced for the second time at the extra passenger, fearful that he had caught the dreadful implication.

The passenger's face also lit up with violent determination. "I'll go with you, Marcella..."

The girl gave a start.

"Jimmie!"

She and the doctor both gasped simultaneously. Her arms went up to him and for the next few minutes the three of them hugged and laughed and cried by turns. It was a welcome wave of gladness in the midst of tragedy. They poured questions to him faster than he could answer, and chided him for sitting so silent and gnome-like through the ride.

They learned of his perilous journey over the coastal mountains with his staunch comrades, Joe and Chumpo. They learned of his flight from Debenz back to Pravianna, which took his last bit of money.

"Then I had just enough cash left to call from the airport. That was noon today, and they told me you'd already left for the Stupodes Show, so I ran all the way. When I found out admittance to the show wasn't free, the best thing I could do was slip in through the back entrances. I finally made it into a room off the arena..." his thrilling tale ended on a somber note, "...where I could see everything."

"Then—you saw?" Marcella asked.

"Yes."

SILENCE fell heavy again. "How'd they ever get Blaine in a fix like that?" the boy finally asked.

The doctor shuffled uncomfortably; he wished to postpone this talk. But Marcella's nerves were strong and her face showed a new fighting spirit.

"We don't know, Jimmie. We only know he went to Africa to fight against this thing—and to find you—"

"He did?" The boy was aghast. "I must have gotten away before he came." A flash came in his mind's eye—the picture of a stranger outside the entrance of the stupodes pen, beating off several guards, leaping over the gate into the swarm of prisoners where the insidious Knockouts lurked

with deadly needles. "Yeah…I guess he came all right. I remember it now. I wouldn't have got out of it hadn't been for him. So they got him instead of me…" Angry tears came into the boy's eyes. "I know who did it! And I'll go back down there and—"

"No, Jimmie," said the doctor sternly. "This is a bigger fight than one man against another. It's a fight of laws and principles. If we ever settle it we'll do it through courts, in a legal manner, not with violence."

"But *Blaine*…" the boy cried. "We can't just hang back after what's happened to Blaine."

"If there was anything on earth we could do—" Defiance was in the doctor's tone, but his words crashed against hopeless barriers. Marcella knew what those barriers were—laws that forbade private physicians to lay hands upon stupodes; even laws that could initiate confiscation of vital materials.

"Doctor Ravenstein," she implored, hoping against hope, "if I brought my husband to you as he is now, would you dare try to help him?"

Ravenstein touched the girl's forehead with compassion. "You're feverish, dear. You'd best put these things out of your mind and rest until—"

"But we'd never let anyone know. Blaine and I would go away—to another country—so you'd never get into any trouble. Would you—could you—for Blaine?"

The venerable old man bit his lips with anguish. He could not bring himself to answer that it was more than laws, it was his own failing skill that prevented such an experiment. He turned his head away.

Marcella closed her eyes, knowing she shouldn't have asked. She only seared her tragic wound with more poignant realization. There were limits to the miracles of science.

But her fighting blood flowed hotly. She could never leave Blaine to such a fate. Whatever the consequences, it was better that she administer a merciful death with her own hands.

"I'm going to get Blaine," she said. "I'm going to free him." Her words were brittle diamonds. "This is my battle now. He's my husband. I'll go for him tonight."

If persuasion failed with Karnairre, she would try purchase, or employ whatever strategy seemed best. The doctor shook his head helplessly. Jimmie, however, was more seasoned to danger.

"I'll go, too, to be sure nothing happens."

"That's swell of you, Jimmie, but—" she doubted whether Karnairre would tolerate an uninvited guest. But Jimmie insisted on going. His bronzed face lit with a latent but mischievous grin.

"I've got the very scheme, right here in this bag." He opened a sack and drew forth a handful of black and white checkered collars. "I found these in a room behind the arena. I was afraid they might fall into dangerous hands so I picked them up—thought they might come in handy. I'll wear one tonight and attend the party as your stupode. No questions asked."

CHAPTER SIX
Peril on the Roof

BLAINE RISING felt weak. He groped mentally. He tried to explain this strange feeling to himself but the thoughts wouldn't come. He needed words to think with, and the words he wanted were always just out of reach.

He plodded across the pebbly roof under the party lights up close to the sky and tried to remember. Why should he be wearing this purple uniform with the gold sash, carrying this tray of drinks to that farther table?

Because someone told him to. That was his reason. Now some people called him to bring the drinks this way instead. He changed his course at once. The people laughed. Amusing to them that he obeyed so well. He didn't like for them to laugh. He wished he could hit them, but something told him he mustn't. He must obey. It was easier. There were already stripes on his body from times he was slow to obey.

Sometimes he groped in his mind for ways to disobey or to resist. But the ideas wouldn't come clear. Before he could grasp them, he would somehow go ahead and carry out the order.

Just like now. He didn't especially want to bring the drinks to these laughing people instead of the others, but he did it. They told him to and he did. He wished he had just one master to obey. It would be easier.

"We put one over on you that time, Karnairre," shouted one of the laughers to the big fat man with the beard who sat at the farther table.

"Your stupodes obey too well," another laugher roared.

Blaine smiled a little and blushed. They seemed to be talking about him. It sounded like a compliment, but words went so fast it was hard to tell.

The fat, black-bearded man at the farther table guffawed. "You're one up on me, Bill, but we'll get the next drinks or I'll make Three-Kay go stick his head down the ventilator." Then the big black bearded man and the others laughed and laughed. All except that certain one. Marcella.

Three-Kay—that was Blaine. There was more to his name. Something like Jay—Three-Kay—Three-Kay. He couldn't remember it all, but it was stamped on his collar. Easier for him when they just called him Three-Kay.

He looked around for the ventilator as he went back to the roof bar for more drinks. But it was hard to remember what a venti—venti—looked like. Then the word escaped him, and there was nothing left except a vague fear that the fat man with the black beard might harm him.

He wished he could hit the big fat man. Maybe he would do it sometime, only the man always shouted something at him and then he felt afraid to hit. Besides, he was so tired. This tiredness didn't seem right somehow. Neither did the fear. Things didn't used to be that way before—

Before what? He couldn't quite think back to *before*. Only a little. It was strongest when he looked at that certain one— Marcella—the pretty one who sat beside the big black-bearded man. Why did she always stare at him with such a frightened look?

He felt warm toward her. There was something about her, and him—he couldn't quite remember.

Maybe she wanted him to say something when she looked at him that way, or maybe not, he couldn't tell which. She seemed so nervous whenever he came near. Once she tipped her drink over. He thought he should go away, but the fat man with the beard called him back for something.

THE party grew louder and more confused. Sometimes Blaine would stop to look at the boy who always favored him with a friendly twinkle. He was Jimmie Br—somebody. Jimmie, at least. It seemed vaguely good that Jimmie should be here, but something about his looks wasn't so good. It was that collar, just like all the waiters wore—including himself.

"Marcella wants to talk with you," Jimmie whispered. "She wants to take you home."

Blaine smiled a little, then went on with his tray.

Jimmie, playing the role of stupode, kept his eyes on Marcella, but she wasn't getting anywhere. He grew restless. Then, as the liquors flowed faster and the roof bar became rushed, good fortune brought him something to relieve the monotony. He overheard the nearby bartenders.

"Henry, if you'd move that robot out of the way, we'd make better time."

"Okay, I'll put him out by the wall. I'd put him to work serving, only you know Karnairre. No robots at his parties. Nothing but stupodes."

"Yeah. Better put him around the corner."

A man-size obelisk of power rolled out of the bartender's door toward Jimmie's corner. The boy was thrilled. No companion could be more welcome. His fingers itched to touch the controls, which he studied in the dim light. But he held back, remembering that no stupode had the intelligence to operate a robot. The temptation was great, but he clasped his fingers behind him, waited, endured, and kept an eye on Marcella.

MARCELLA starved for a chance to talk with Blaine. Every minute was torture for her. She neither drank nor jested, but somehow she led Karnairre on. He loved to boast of his startling career, his stony-heartedness. No use to appeal for Blaine's return. There wasn't an ounce of sympathy in the man's make-up. Blaine, to him, was simply something to command, something to whip when the mood struck him, eventually something to sell. Marcella was desperate.

The others at her table listened as the great executive unfolded his arrogant plans to expand his industry.

"Confidentially," he gloated, "I've got the Confederation eating right out of my hand. In two years I'll flood this country with stupodes." He tilted his beard with gusto.

"Have you talked it over with the Superior Court?" Marcella dared to ask.

The forthcoming Superior Court battle was a thorn in his flesh, but his magniloquent mood dulled the pain.

"Superior—say, Beautiful, I've got those judges packed away right in my pockets." He suited antics to words. "Here's Grayson in this pocket, and Tempera in this pocket, and—"

"Don't run out of pockets," someone said. "Seven judges you know."

"But it only takes four to say the word. I've got them lined up as regular as the seasons. Never doubt it, the great Karnairre has tricks up his sleeve."

Some skeptic across the table gave the conversation a fearful turn. "What about that fracas at the show this afternoon? Any tricks for that?"

The bearded man scowled. Marcella went faint, closed her eyes, and held on breathless. But no one noticed. The heckler pursued the point.

"The papers are full of it. They're takin' the stupode industry for a ride—and just wait till they find the girl... What a story she'll give 'em."

"They won't find her if I find her first," Karnairre said with a surly laugh. "I'll teach her to mind her manners."

"Yeah?"

"Yeah. Whenever women come to me weeping for their menfolk, I threaten to turn them over to the Uplift Board to face the exams themselves. That usually cools them off."

"Who you s'pose that girl was?"

"I don't know," Karnairre growled. "Who gives a damn?"

"You might if you'd seen it the way it came over television. Didn't look so good for the stupode business. In fact, my friend, it looked worse than that."

"Aw, quit gripin'," said the skeptic's girl friend. "I wanna drink an' I wanna dance an' I don't wanna hear no more of your blabbin'."

"Excuse me," said Marcella, and she fled.

"There—see!" said the girl friend. "She's sick of your blabbin' too."

"Let her go," said Karnairre. He rose and went the other way.

MARCELLA'S heart beat madly. She sought the shadows—anywhere to escape.

There was Blaine by the wall. At last, the chance her heart had cried for.

"Blaine, dear," she caught him. The lights were dim. No one would see her smother him in a feverish embrace. "Blaine, dear, I've been dying for you to come back... Talk to me, Blaine. Tell me you're all right."

A little of the girl's hysterical emotion went to him. "I'm kind of...all right—"

"What have they done to you? Don't look away, Blaine. Talk to me. Do you remember things—or—"

"I remember you...you're Marcella."

"Oh, Blaine…" She buried her sobs against his chest, then shook his shoulders with trembling hands, tried to draw responses from him. His words were brief and simple, his emotions negligible.

"Blaine…can't you *make* yourself be different? Don't be afraid of the whip. Don't be afraid of anything. Get a grip on yourself, Blaine. Use your *will power!*"

Blaine smiled uncomfortably and murmured, "What do you want me…to do?"

Marcella gave way to a torrent of tears. How futile to plead for will power when the glands were too sluggish from drugs to supply any initiative. The stoppage of a fraction of an ounce of life-driving chemicals made all the difference. No magic of mind over matter could make up for it.

And still the suggestion was not entirely lost; Blaine struggled to grasp the situation.

A warning *hiss* came from Jimmie. Marcella stepped back, her mind whirling dizzily.

"What's going on here?" Karnairre thundered. "Choosing the company of stupodes in preference to me?" He laughed harshly. "Trying to make me jealous?" He jested, but there was a note of suspicion in his questions.

Marcella applied her powder puff and turned to him.

"This stupode—er—"

"Not annoying you, was he?" His words cut sharp.

"No—oh, no! I was just—looking him over. I wish to buy him. What's the price?"

Karnairre's look of suspicion relaxed. He expected to raffle off a few stupodes later in the night, but a sale was a sale.

"Come out in the light and we'll see what he looks like."

"I'll buy him here and now," said Marcella. She snatched at her pocketbook, handed him a bill. "I'll arrange to pay the rest later. I must leave at once."

"Hold on here." Karnairre's appetite turned from the commercial to the romantic as he pocketed the bill. "Not so early in the evening. I've...taken a fancy to you."

With no thought of the checkered collar that hovered near, or the younger stupode parked by the wall, he took Marcella's hands. Dim lights, a pretty girl, a moment of seclusion. He tried to embrace her.

A strange thing happened. The stupode she had just bought stepped in and pushed Karnairre away. The huge man gasped in amazement. "What the hell—"

"Mine!" asserted Blaine. A dim sense of possession moved him.

The great Karnairre gasped in a surprised tone. "Why you damned—" He whipped out a lash and drew it back to strike. The girl stifled a cry and caught his arm. Then, as if to paralyze him with astonishment, the stupode said, "I want to hit you." A fist shot out.

Physically the blow was staggering enough. But the psychological effect was a cold knockout. Karnairre's universe tottered. The whole stupodes industry trembled to the roots. A jealous stupode!

The shocked man leaped forward. His eyes nearly blazed. His whip arm raised. Down came the lash in seven swift cutting strokes across Blaine's body. Upraised for the eighth—

It did not descend. Steel arms prevented him. A robot's automatic grip seized up the huge body of Karnairre, held him aloft, powerless to do more than kick and cry.

"This way!" Jimmie shouted, snatching something from the robot. He and Marcella caught Blaine's hands. They slipped back of the roof bar and gained the exit, hesitated a moment to look back and were frozen momentarily by the sight.

Karnairre's struggle had started the robot coasting. The crowd awoke to his cry; several started after him with terrified screams. The robot accelerated down the gently inclined roof toward the far edge. Feet thudded after it.

But the sprinters' efforts were wasted. When the automatic mechanism came to the danger point, its safety devices checked it; suction feet went down to hold it fast. High in its arms the great Karnairre overhung the roof's edge, safe as the famous leaning tower, to glare with bulging eyes at the lighted street hundreds of feet below.

Blaine and his escorts scurried into an elevator.

CHAPTER SEVEN
A Fighting Stupode

THE candid shot, which some enterprising cameraman caught of the frightened Karnairre perched over the roof's edge like a wild-eyed gargoyle, created a sensation. Between television and the newspapers, the whole nation saw it. A splendid study in facial expression. The great executive with his picturesque beard was a popular camera subject anyway. To see him thus struggling in the embrace of his arch-competitor, the mechanical robot, tickled the public fancy.

Reports varied as to the facts back of the picture. Some accounts insisted that a stupode had set off the mischievous robot. Karnairre's rebuff was that the whole scene was a set-up by his competitors. Many superstitious persons who liked to believe that robots had the power to think and choose, seized on the rumor that this mechanical man intended to murder his sworn enemy.

But aside from the scalding ridicule it brought Karnairre, the incident's chief effect was to remind the public of the deep underlying conflict between two rising industries: mechanical robots and human robots—stupodes.

A few days later a more serious story broke—the answer to the mystery of the girl involved in the scene at the Stupodes Show the previous week.

The story bombshelled across the continent. The girl was none other than the former Marcella Kingman, now Marcella Rising, one of the three Americans who had made headlines a few months earlier by their spectacular return to life from a previous century. The public remembered, and read her story avidly.

She told everything, from Jimmie's disappearance, to her own purchase of her ill-fated husband, to Karnairre's use of the Whip. There were pictures to illustrate the latter scene, for Jimmie had programmed the robot's infrared camera to operate during the last few minutes on the roof and had snatched the film before leaving.

Thus, sound pictures carried the heart-rending drama to the people. Marcella telecast her personal appeal against the stupode evil, for she was sure that public opinion, the ultimate power in any nation, could find an answer. Her appeal rang true. Thousands turned their attention to the stupode scandal for the first time and felt vaguely that they should do something about it.

But one question the interviewers asked most often, Marcella evaded. "What has happened to your husband, Mrs. Rising? Won't you let us see him? The television audience would like for him to say a few words—"

"Please…" Marcella would answer, turning her head away. "He is gone. That's all I can say."

The Rising incident still lingered in the hearts of the people when the fall session of the Superior Court took the spotlight. At last…a test case. Perhaps the stupodes industry would be found illegal in its overall nature. Perhaps stupodes would be declared human and deserving of the rights thereof.

THE outer world as well as the Central European Confederation looked on eagerly and grew tense as the hearings began. Was the Superior Court prepared to strike a deathblow to the checkered collar traffic, or leave a clear field for the booming human robot industry?

Fortunes were literally in the balance. Investors and gamblers played a nervous game while they waited for the hand of the Superior Court to point in a final direction. The frenzied stockholders of the Stupodes Corporation swarmed after Karnairre, demanding to know whether he could save them from financial disaster. He came back at them with courteous ridicule of their fears—he had plenty of trumps up his sleeve.

"Don't let all of this go to your heads," he said tersely at a stockholders' meeting. "The future of the stupode program is completely secure. Four of the judges line up with us on almost every legal issue. Put your minds at rest."

Karnairre knew. Four of the seven dignitaries came to the daily hearings with their minds fairly well decided in advance.

But the judges were only human. They saw the pendulum of public sympathies swinging in the other direction. The Blaine Rising affair had thrown the nation's attitude into and entirely different direction. No need to launch a decision squarely against the tide of popular whimsy—better delay action for the time being and give public sentiment time to swing back.

One of the judges then became conveniently ill and the hearings were postponed.

Tension among Karnairre's employees and stockholders relaxed a bit. Their interest soon returned to the weekly and monthly sales charts.

But no one relaxed in the presence of the great J. Karl Karnairre. He had the jitters, and the court's delay didn't give him any comfort. Since the Rising affair, Karnairre kept an amber colored demijohn of whiskey on his ebony desk. As the company sales went down, so did the level of the whiskey. Interestingly, though, sales had briefly jumped to a peak, but then plummeted again. The spike in sales had happened the week after the Rising woman's first releases to the press. Every time Karnairre's eyes fell on that sharp peak in sales, it gave him pause. It didn't make sense to him at first—nearly a thousand unexpected sales at a precise moment in time that one would have expected a slump.

Something seemed amiss.

All that had been several weeks before. But the reasons for the abnormal peak in sales had never really been fully explained, in spite of Karnairre's repeated requests to his staff—and it preyed on his mind, like a slow torture within him. He tried to quench it with whiskey.

Now Karnarrie sat—one hand on the demijohn, eyes on the chart—waiting for his staff to come in for their weekly meeting. His secretaries and department heads seated themselves around the table, prepared for what were sure to be wrathful comments.

Karnairre began with a courteous but to-the-point tongue-lashing of the sales staff. Sales were off drastically from normal levels. Secondly, in all the weeks since, no one on the staff had come up with a full clarification for the one week of abnormally high sales.

NEXT he turned on Smitt because the secret service bureau had never located Blaine Rising. A fighting stupode running about loose—what a wonderful advertisement for business that was.

"I've got our best agents on the lookout," Smitt said firmly in his defense. "We've got three men keeping watch on Ravenstein's home. Rising's wife is there. She'll lead us to him...sooner or later."

"I think he's dead," someone spoke up. "The newspapers printed an anonymous account about a mercy killing shortly after she purchased him, and the way she's keeping mum might lead one to believe that—"

"Don't be fooled by her," Karnairre snapped. "Rising's alive. And if there's an underground movement, she's in on it. She's a very clever individual under that pouty exterior."

"You ought to know," cracked Judson under his breath.

"That's enough, Judson," Karnairre snarled under his breath. His dictatorial grip had slipped since the roof party.

"What's the latest information on this underground movement?" asked Lemska. "Just more newspaper talk?"

"That's what I'm getting at," Karnairre blustered. He jerked his thumb toward the primary sales chart. "That abnormal jump came right after the public image black eye we received over of the whole Rising affair. It's my educated guess that a high percentage of the stupode transactions we got during that spike in sales went into the hands of doctors."

"Doctors? Why doctors?" Lemska asked.

Karnairre paused before answering.

"...*For treatment.*"

The big perspiring man paused for a drink. He caught Lemska's skeptical look. "So you think I'm jumping to conclusions? Well...maybe it's high time we jumped. During that same week, Smitt's informants saw many strangers coming and going from Dr. Ravenstein's. Professional looking men. Undoubtedly doctors. Sometimes a dozen or more of them at a time. And when Smitt's agents finally detained one of them, what did they find on him? A small bottle of unlabeled medicine—*unlabeled.*"

"Containing what?"

"Yes...*what?* The agents weren't fast enough to stop him from grabbing the bottle back, leaping to the curb, and pouring its contents into a storm water drain. That night they raided Ravenstein's secret laboratories and found them cleaned out—nothing. So there we are. But that tells us a story. Ravenstein turned rebellious when the Uplift Act was originally enacted. He's been working up hormone cultures these past few years to be ready when he and his followers finally got a chance to try them on the stupode population."

Some of the executives at the table stared silently with expressions of surprise, even disbelief on their faces. This was why Karnairre had been in such an agitated state. The industry was over a legal fire, but too much heat could blow the entire industry sky high, laws and all. The shadow of the Rising incident fell onto Ravenstein's doorstep. Ravenstein and his fellow doctors were out for blood.

"Who was the brilliant person who slipped Blaine Rising into the stupode factory in the first place?" Smitt asked.

"Or dozens of others like him?" Lemska added.

Judson jumped to his own defense. "I tried to tell you here in a meeting one day, Karnairre, and you wouldn't—"

"Sit down…" Karnairre interrupted forcefully. The others at the table froze. He eyed them all with his old sense of power and jumped quickly to a decision.

"We'll recall all stupodes from that specific sales period…to check them over," he growled softly. "The law allows us to do this. Get every registration number that went out that week. That's within our legal rights—and they have to comply. It'll give us a chance to derail this underground movement before it gains any real momentum."

Lemska was critical. "To recall nearly a thousand stupodes will look horrible from a sales standpoint."

But Karnairre seized on a coming national holiday. "We'll also call them in for the Liberation Day parade. Pay their expenses. Most of the public won't suspect a thing."

"And if their owners don't comply…?"

"Then we'll have to make sure that they *do* comply," the president said steely. "We'll send agents out to make sure of it. You can't hide a thousand stupodes for long. Current laws won't offer the doctors any legal recourse. Legally, they have to comply."

The group sat in complacent silence for several moments. Perhaps stupode stocks would rise again soon. Whether the nearly one thousand stupodes bought for experimental purposes by Ravenstein and his associates were kept in hiding, or whether they were sent forth to the Liberation Day celebration, the underground anti-stupode movement would hopefully be derailed.

Smitt indiscreetly spoke up to shatter the pretty picture. "But suppose the doctors *could* change stupodes back into functional human beings? And suppose they actually succeeded and have a few?"

Some in the group glared at Smitt.

He continued on, though. "Would the former stupodes remember things that happened while they *were* stupodes? For example, would this fighting stupode, Blaine Rising, remember all he saw down in the African laboratories?"

A chill shot through the conference. Karnairre paled and poured himself another drink with unsteady hands.

"Blaine Rising's dead," someone muttered, trying to derail Smitt's negative comments.

"I don't know—" Smitt said doubtfully.

"We'd better find out," Karnairre rasped. "Have your men redouble their efforts—leave no stone unturned. Who knows, maybe our friend Mr. Rising will meet with an accident of some kind—an accident that doesn't look too suspicious. I give you one more week…"

To everyone's surprise, the door suddenly opened and three of Smitt's men dragged themselves in, all of them a disheveled mess. One had a split lip, the other two wore purple swollen eyes.

"Blaine Rising is back," said one of them through swollen lips. "He's at Ravenstein's."

"Why didn't you bring him in?" Karnairre flashed.

"Why didn't we? Because that damn stupode's a fighter!"

CHAPTER EIGHT
A Thousand Dangerous Men

MARCELLA looked up into the understanding eyes of her husband. Tears streaked her cheeks. "Don't mind me," she said, laughing and sobbing at the same time. "I'm so happy to have you back. After all you've been through—"

"We won't even think about it." Blaine smiled and held her tightly. "It must have been far worse for you than me."

"You—you remember?"

"Perfectly." He dropped her into the divan and sat beside her. "I wasn't unconscious. I was just slow, sluggish. I couldn't catch the meanings of things until they were gone—but now everything comes back clear—like reading your own diary." He grinned at Jimmie who stood by beaming. "Even to that fast one you and the robot slipped over on Karnairre. I'm going to buy you a robot of your own, Jimmie."

He turned to Ravenstein. The lines of purpose had grown deeper in the kindly old face, but a proud smile glowed.

"Doctor, I wouldn't have believed that your medical friends could change me back to my old self so quickly." He tossed his stupode's collar onto the table. "Guess I'm through with that. Your medicine and those brilliant physicians you turned me over to—"

Ravenstein's warning gesture reminded him to talk lower. The doctor muttered, "We scarcely dare breathe around here anymore."

Blaine understood. He knew all about the cooperative scheme of the doctors—to reconstruct nearly a thousand stupodes with Ravenstein's serums. "I hope it isn't too late for me to help with the movement," he said.

"I'm ready for you to take over the active leadership," said the doctor. The greatest task is still ahead—the task of humanizing these poor souls who have always been under the control of Karnairre's corporation—who are now in possession of normal human capacities for thinking and behaving, for the first time in their lives.

Blaine did not underestimate this task. Marcella and Jimmie agreed with him that—much as they yearned for America—they wouldn't return to their home country until they had devoted a full year to Ravenstein's humanitarian revolution. If they could mentally transform the experimental stupodes into normal persons—and somehow convince the public that these creatures were no longer the tail end of the human procession—then with good luck they might undermine the entire stupode industry. It was a colossal, unromantic task, but Ravenstein's three guests faced it determinedly and accepted the challenge, never guessing that the ultimate clash was only two short weeks away.

"It was you and Marcella who started the movement rolling," said the doctor. "Within twenty-four hours after your wife's first public appeal, scores of doctors informed us they were ready to back us. But we'll have a long fight on our hands. And Karnairre's tactics—"

"Blaine!" Marcella suddenly gasped as she saw his bruised knuckles. "You've—you've been in a fight...?"

"Guilty," Blaine laughed. "Some thugs were laying for me as I came in. They thought I was still a stupode. Of course, legally, I suppose I still am."

His chuckle went cold as he felt a feeling of trepidation fall upon the group. It suddenly came home to them that he had cleared only one hurdle. Others waited—insidious unseen dangers—legal traps—lawless thugs.

The doctor bit his lips. "You're in their spotlight, Blaine. There's nothing they fear more than a thinking, fighting stupode. And what Karnairre fears, he strives to stamp out."

A grimmer thought came to Blaine. "By this time, legally speaking, there are about a thousand fighting stupodes. A thousand that have suddenly come into possession of all their natural human impulses—and most of them have never had any training in applying the brakes! A thousand brand new, fully-grown humans. Until we get them a little educated they may well be, in a very real sense, dangerous men. We've got to keep them under cover until they've had enough time to get used to their newfound mental and emotional skills—or this whole thing could blow up in our faces..."

There was a moment of cold silence, then something battered loudly at the rear of the house.

THEY found a wounded, gasping stranger slumped against the back door. Blaine carried his bloody form to a nearby bed. Ravenstein applied first aid to the bullet wounds while the stranger talked swiftly against ebbing time. Smitt's men had scuffled with him and shot him, leaving him in an alley to die after driving away in a black automobile.

"I have to tell you what they're planning," he moaned. "Maybe I'm a traitor, but Karnairre never gave me the chance I deserved. I've taken enough off him to last a lifetime. I'm on his staff. Name's Judson."

The little group stood rigid above him as he poured forth Karnairre's plans: an accidental death for Blaine and a surprise re-call for nearly a thousand stupodes shortly before the Liberation Day parade.

When the ambulance came, Blaine, Jimmie, and the doctor's robot also went along for the ride. It was their chance to slip out quickly and safely. No time to waste now. Nearly a thousand new "men" would soon be put to the test.

A year's training must be compressed into two weeks. As Ravenstein's newly appointed leader of the movement, Blaine knew it was up to him to personally touch base with as many of the former stupodes and their doctors as possible before Liberation Day. Ravenstein shook his head dubiously as the ambulance slid off into the darkness.

Not too much later, Blaine, Jimmie, and the robot had boarded a private plane and were flying out of the area. The lights of Pravianna receded as their plane sped them on their way. The nearly one thousand former stupodes were scattered all over the Central European Confederation. To make the rounds would require dozens of stops. Blaine made his plans down to the minute. The two of them would go day and night, sleeping only between stops. His special robot pilot was dependable—without need of sleep or nourishment. Every doctor would be ready with his stupodes. Marcella would alert them by telephone to Blaine's impending arrival.

BLAINE stood before a cluster of ten stupodes gathered in one of the doctors' homes. He saw the eager curiosity in their faces. They were still in their initial phase of re-exploring life through new eyes of understanding. For thirty minutes he rolled out his swift advice to them...

The fate of all stupodes depended upon them...

They must prepare for Liberation Day. They must be models of self-discipline. They must not let Karnairre's men know they had been treated by physicians. For that one specific day they must pretend to be dumbly obedient—even if someone should crack a whip at them.

They must stick together...

Behave with restraint, and keep their stupode collars on. However, if anyone should line them up for medication or blood tests or try to close them into a room, they must rebel, escape, and come back to their doctors.

Blaine patted them on the shoulders, shook their hands. Jimmie had been making audio recordings of each briefing. He handed one to the doctor on the way out.

Over the next several days, the stupodes' time was taken up by rapid-fire education, doctors' lectures, Blaine's recorded instructions and advice, discussions, and practice in restrained manners. Even as the stupodes slept, earphones leading from a continuously repeating recording kept up the constant bombardment of admonitions and warnings, planting them deeply within their subconscious minds.

Blaine and the doctors saw the reconstructed stupodes for what they really were—children in the bodies of adults. Two weeks of training would hardly be sufficient. It would take years of living. But two weeks would have to be enough.

The former stupodes smiled upon Blaine at his visits. They studied his manner curiously, but were diverted by trifles. They were still in the stage of elemental wants. They quarreled over clothing, grabbed for candy, rushed to the windows as females passed by on the streets. For the first time in their lives, they were filled with anxiety and boldness.

The constant lecturing about conducting themselves in such a way that might lead to the freedom of other stupodes often fell on shallow ground. Many of these "new" humans wanted to eat, to play, to possess, to make things with their hands, to compete with each other—and not be too concerned with much else.

But Blaine was unfailingly persistent and his words eventually seemed to get through to them. During the briefings, the robot projected the sound film of Blaine's physical confrontation with Karnairre on the rooftop. As Blaine's fist struck out, the stupodes roared with delight, but when the big man's whip went into action, they sobered. Old memories stirred.

They began to understand...

CHAPTER NINE
Liberation Day

"LADIES and gentlemen of the television audience, it's Liberation Day!" the announcer boomed. "A hundred and twenty years since the overthrow of the dictators—and what a day. All Pravianna dressed up to celebrate! People already gathering in the stadium, bands marching on Grand Parade Street, colors flying. There'll be many a flashy uniform and spectacular float on Grand Parade Street today. We see a company of infantry going by at this moment. Farther up the street, several war machines. Beyond them we can glimpse a shining regiment of robots, all operated by a single control...

"Now let's look at these flashy purple and gold uniforms gathering on the edge of Parade Park. Checkered collars and banners tells us these fine looking stupodes are from the 3-K series..."

Marcella stood close to the televisor and scanned the face of every checkered collar she could see. Blaine must be mixed in with them somewhere. He and Jimmie and the robot had left in a taxi some two hours before.

The sound of a telephone ringing broke her concentration. Dr. Ravenstein picked up the hallway receiver, out of earshot of Marcella.

"Hello? Jimmie?"

After a brief conversation the doctor set the receiver down again and took a deep breath. Blaine and Jimmie had escaped an attempt on their lives. They had now left their taxi and were proceeding to the Parade park as quickly as possible on foot.

Ravenstein slumped into a chair, withholding the news from Marcella, who was already worried sick.

The doctor tried to tell himself that Blaine and Jimmie would somehow live through the end of the Liberation Day festivities. For two weeks the two of them had worked like demons to prepare for this day—perhaps only to be slain by paid murderers. The minutes dragged on.

The television announcer's voice suddenly struck a jarring note. "It now appears there's been an accident—an accident down one of the side streets very near to us. We couldn't catch it on camera, it happened so quickly. There…now you can see it—over there where the crowd's gathering. It appears that a large business sign that was hanging over the street suddenly ripped loose and fell to the ground, and it may have struck some pedestrians below. We'll be close enough to see in just a few moments."

The announcer and his cameraman moved through the crowd toward the accident scene.

"It appears there may be a couple of victims. One is apparently a teenage boy and the other is…well the other appears to have been a robot. If you look up you can see broken bits of hanging chain that appear to have been holding the sign. It's impossible to say, but perhaps the overall noise of the parade, or even the vibrations of parade marchers may have jarred it loose from its moorings. It made an incredible sound when it hit.

"And now we can see that someone else was also under the falling sign. Why…why it appears to be a stupode. In fact…he seems to be administering first aid to the teenage boy!" The announcer chuckled under his breath at this. "Well there's a first for Mr. Karnairre's product line—a stupode that can administer first aid…

"Now you can see—bring the camera a bit closer—that the boy is breathing and his eyes appear to be half-open."

There was a brief pause before the announcer continued.

"Someone has just whispered in my ear that they saw the robot's arms go up as the sign fell, as though to catch it, otherwise both the boy and the stupode would have probably been crushed... And here comes an ambulance now! As you can probably hear, the people around the scene are now applauding for this young man, who appears not to have been too badly injured. He seems to be whispering something into the stupode's ear as he's being loaded into the ambulance... We'll try to get a closer shot of the stup—but wait—"

The attending stupode suddenly rose and walked straight through the crowd, away from the camera.

The announcer chuckled under his breath again. "Well there he goes. I guess we won't get a closer shot after all, folks. As you can see the stupode has abruptly—and very quickly I might add—left the accident scene. He's bolted right through the crowd into that swarm of stupodes beyond.

"And now, as we swing back to the accident scene, you can see that some in the crowd are gathering in around the crushed robot—apparently picking up pieces of it for souvenirs. Well this was certainly a bad start for somebody's big day. We'd love to get a few words from Mr. Karnairre about all this, but we've been told the well-known stupodes king is busy with an important conference this morning..."

PRESIDENT KARNAIRRE perspired as two judges of the Superior Court faced him in his sanctum sanctorum. A great honor, but the pressure was oppressive, with a thousand unpredictable stupodes on his mind.

The judges were obviously worried. There was incredible pressure on them to issue a final ruling on the stupodes case. The public clamored for a decision.

"Yes…" Karnairre thundered in a low, intense voice, "…the instant you release your final decision I'm sure the public will embrace it."

Both judges certainly hoped so, but they clung to doubts. A fair but safe judgment was paramount. And they had themselves to consider as well.

Karnairre methodically went over the practical as well as the legal considerations. Stupendous investments made the checkered collar industry a cornerstone of prosperity. The judges seemed to be weighing the factors carefully, pondering long upon the glories of the Uplift regime. After Karnairre finished speaking with them, both judges shook his hand and took their leave.

As soon as their honors were halfway down the corridor that insulated Karnairre's private office from his battery of secretaries, the stupodes magnate snatched up the telephone and called a number of important stockholders to give the account of his conversation with the judges.

But one of the adjudicators, Judge Tempero, discovered he had forgotten his notebook and started back. He stopped before the closed door to hear Karnairre's voice thunder, "I've got these judicial saps eating out of my hand."

Tempero made it a rule never to break dignity, but his legal mind reasoned that one may eavesdrop with perfect dignity. Judge Grayson, following him back, concurred in this opinion. As they listened, they were shocked by profuse references to their pedigrees. They faced each other with a new understanding of Karnairre, and even themselves.

The two judges, now with grim expressions on their faces, continued listening. They heard someone come in from another door, whom Karnairre received cordially.

"Hello Mr. Karnairre." A voice sounded.

"Well, Braba my friend, it's good to see you."

"You, too, sir."

"You've had a chance to look over the J-3's?"

"Yes, sir."

"Then tell me flatly, do you think these doctors have done them any damage?"

"I can't see it in their actions. They're surprisingly quiet and orderly, even for stupodes. We'll have to give them complete physical examinations before we can tell—"

"There's really no time for that now. As garish as this may sound, test them with the whip. If they show the slightest signs of fighting back, lock them up securely."

"Then what?"

"We'll give them an operation that no doctor in the world can undo."

"And if they don't fight back?"

"Then you'll know they're still untouched stupodes. Watch them closely, though. If they really haven't been tampered with, we may as well get them into the parade for the advertising. Send them once around Grand Parade Street at three o'clock. I'll be on hand to announce them as they circle through the stadium."

Braba went out the way he had come. Karnairre poured himself a drink and pondered over the ease with which he had "ironed" things out. Plenty sweet, the way those J-3's had been gathered in at Pravianna on such short notice. If the owners had any illegal business up their sleeves, they still had a healthy fear of the stupode king's legal rights.

Judges Tempero and Grayson forgot the missing notebook, tiptoed their way out of the building with light-footed dignity, and taxied off.

STRONG hearted though Marcella was, paralyzing fear bore down upon her. The fates were closing in swiftly. Jimmie's nerve shattering ordeal—hidden treacheries that waited for Blaine—it was almost too much to endure.

The doctor shared her terrors. Blaine's plight was doubly perilous. If he should be singled out of the swarm of stupodes, caught whispering directions to them, he would lose his freedom, and they, their cause.

When Jimmie's broken wrists were set and bandaged and the ugly gash over his shoulder stitched, the heroic lad slipped off into a deep sleep.

Marcella returned to the televisor and tuned her eyes to catch everything that passed. Ravenstein saw her lips tremble and begged her to come away, but she wouldn't. She flinched as she saw Braba wield the Whip. She knew every stroke was a spark glancing off dynamite. One by one the ex-stupodes passed the test and took the cutting blows like the simple stupodes they used to be.

The waiting line shuffled along. Blaine came onto the screen. She quivered. She, too, felt the rage that must have tore within him at the very sight of Lieutenant Braba. Blaine had often spoke of Braba; the stupodes show; the lash that had made her cry out. Next to Karnairre it was Braba who most aroused Blaine and Marcella's loathing.

A faint chill swept through her. If Blaine was whipped, would he take it without striking back? She thought not. He would leap like a madman, wreak his vengeance on the spot. And yet, she realized, one break would release a thousand undisciplined creatures upon the despised authorities. Then—a riot of blood—and a lost cause.

Blaine was next.

The television announcer turned back to the street to divert his audience with more pleasant scenes. Blaine and the stupodes were gone from the screen. Marcella closed her eyes.

Late that afternoon the checkered collars came back to the television audience as they marched into view at the stadium. The telecaster flashed about from one parading group to another. Then as the full body of purple and gold uniforms moved onto the circular track, the announcer turned the microphone over to Karnairre, who had something to say about the 2090 model stupodes as a manifestation of national progress.

The stadium crowd immediately grew attentive, not to Karnairre's words, but to the strange behavior of the marching stupodes the instant his voice began to boom through the speakers.

Every ex-stupode recognized that voice. Some of them began to mumble and point. That was the same black-bearded man who had lashed Blaine in the short film they had all seen. Blaine was their friend. They resented that lashing.

Yes, that was the very man, standing on the little platform near their path like a puffing boiler. Now only a few yards away. There was no one near him now except the television man and a few photographers. "I could smack him..." one of them muttered. An officer's whip cracked without effect.

It was too tempting. Blaine's whispered orders, "Keep marching! Look straight ahead!" continued to grapevine through the ranks. Still, the marchers edged toward Karnairre magnetically.

"Keep marching!" Blaine cried out. His frantic words carried to the microphones. Earnest words, but they were lost against Karnairre's irritating bluster. A thousand stupodes hated that voice. Moreover, a thousand resistances had run low. Being lashed, keeping quiet, parading, looking straight ahead, passing stands where the smell of popcorn teased them, holding in like model stupodes for hours—it was all too much. Children that they were, they demanded action. They couldn't hold back any longer.

A tall ungainly creature named Big John led off by shouting, "That's the guy I want to meet…and push his face in."

"Me, too."

"Yeah…he needs it."

"Let's smear him up a little…"

"No. No! *NO!*" Blaine shouted, but his voice was lost.

A rush of purple and gold uniforms, checkered collars. Whips flashed. The officers couldn't strike fast enough to turn the stampede.

KARNAIRRE saw what was coming. His hand flew up in amazement. He was never without his own Whip. He knew how to use it and when. Without a moments' indecision he knew this wasn't one of the proper times. Had he carried a gun, he might have faced the onslaught; but commanders of stupodes were never supposed to need guns.

He leaped heavily from the platform, tried to make an open field run for safety. But Big John tackled him and he went down with a thud. In a split second a dozen ex-stupodes pounced on him. Five seconds more and he was at the bottom of the biggest dog pile ever released to the world through television.

The photographers sprang nimbly to make the most of the scene and still keep a safe distance. The nearly one thousand uniformed creatures pressed toward the center of action. Armed police ran across the field to fight their way into the swarm.

In the seething heaped-up center, whips could be seen lashing at the writhing mass of arms and legs. The vast crowds of the stadium—watching from their tiptoes—were too startled to shout. Had the checkered collars been seized by a mania? The whips did no good. Cries of wild, childish delight came from the focal center. More stupodes leaped onto the heap as fast as others crawled off.

It was a stupode—Blaine Rising—whose commands eventually made the aggressors unpile. Karnairre reappeared, looking more dead than alive, more undressed than dressed. His hair and beard were caked with soil. The pressing thousand edged back to make a small open circle about him. He wobbled to his feet and looked around like the survivor of an avalanche.

Utterly deflated as he was, his wits hadn't been crushed out entirely. He blubbered for a microphone. The television announcer plowed through to him and handed him one.

"This is Mr. Karnairre…telling you what happened…" his choked voice came through the speakers. An amused roar came back at him from the stadium.

"Meddlers did this…" he rasped out. Then, pointing to the stupodes, he continued, "This gang of wild, soft-brained hooligans used to be decent stupodes until they fell into the hands of meddling doctors who tried to turn them into human beings. But it can't be done! This proves it once and for all—"

Blaine grabbed the microphone and flung the huge man back. "It proves nothing! These 'hooligans' as you call them have just started a new life. They now have mental and emotional abilities they never had before. Give them time…"

Karnairre plunged at Blaine. The shadow of their clash fell upon the television receiver. With a steel arm, Blaine held the blustering Karnairre at arm's length.

How he craved to swing a fist at that arrogant jaw!

But he couldn't. A thousand eager ex-stupodes watched. He was their model, and his every act cut a deep pattern in their impressionable minds.

Warning shots sounded from the edge of the mob. Terror spread through the stadium as armed police broke a path toward the center. If those irresponsible creatures should lunge for the policemen's guns…

And they did.

Shrieking with delight, they went for the armed men as if it were a game…

A GUN flew through the air and fell into the open center before the television receiver. It lay there on the ground, and to the utter amazement of the many spectators, no stupode even leaped for it.

"Never shoot a gun!" Blaine shouted. A hundred hilarious voices echoed the slogan. "Never shoot a gun!" The words had been planted through the endless repetition of an audio recording.

Another firearm came whirling through the air to land within the widening arena walled by purple and gold uniforms. Other revolvers followed as they were taken from the hopelessly outnumbered police. The audience looked on in a state of disbelief.

Soon the cry of *"Never shoot a gun!"* rose in volume, and suddenly a thousand voices got off on a rollicking singsong chant.

"Never… Never… Never shoot a gun!
"Never let ourselves get into trouble!
"Never strike an officer. Never hit and run!
"Never fight or quarrel among each other…"

It was a weird turn, from violence to a song of restraint.

The crowd listened dumbfounded. The television audience saw in Blaine's countenance a curious smile. They saw the bewildered Karnairre standing in the center of this strange ritual, unconsciously holding his clothes together with one hand, picking the mud out of his beard with the other. Officers looked on helplessly, as if to say, how can you deal with men that stop in the middle of a fight to speak of peace?

The chanters then went straight through the words of the audio recording without a break. With the closing lines they felt the urge to illustrate words with actions:

"We want liberation! We want human rights!

"We want liberation! We want human rights!

"When we master every rule that governs the human race...

"We'll throw our checkered collars back—in Karnairre's face!"

They unlocked their collars and started to throw. Karnairre bunched to the ground and wrapped his arms over his head. Officers dashed through the checkered snowstorm to protect him.

Wild with exhilaration, the stupodes began to run around in circles. A big voice from the loud speakers brought them to attention.

"Special bulletin! The Superior Court brings us a Liberation Day surprise by rendering a decision in the stupodes case. In a five-to-two vote, the judges declare several sections of the Uplift Act null and void. In substance, they declare that stupodes are legally human, and their manufacture and sale is illegal..."

DR. RAVENSTEIN'S face, glowing with happiness and pride, was the last sight Blaine and Marcella remembered seeing as they zoomed off in an airliner for America. His words of deep gratitude clung in their minds.

They were a part of the new world now, by every right, and great happiness was theirs.

Across the aisle Jimmie groaned. His happiness would come a week hence, when the bandages came off his hands. Until then he would have to exist in patient agony, unable to touch the brand new 2090 model robot that stood beside him.

THE END

If you've enjoyed this book, you will not want to miss these terrific titles...

ARMCHAIR SCI-FI, FANTASY, & HORROR DOUBLE NOVELS, $12.95 each

D-1   **THE GALAXY RAIDERS** by William P. McGivern
       SPACE STATION #1 by Frank Belknap Long

D-2   **THE PROGRAMMED PEOPLE** by Jack Sharkey
       SLAVES OF THE CRYSTAL BRAIN by William Carter Sawtelle

D-3   **YOU'RE ALL ALONE** by Fritz Leiber
       THE LIQUID MAN by Bernard C. Gilford

D-4   **CITADEL OF THE STAR LORDS** by Edmund Hamilton
       VOYAGE TO ETERNITY by Milton Lesser

D-5   **IRON MEN OF VENUS** by Don Wilcox
       THE MAN WITH ABSOLUTE MOTION by Noel Loomis

D-6   **WHO SOWS THE WIND...** by Rog Phillips
       THE PUZZLE PLANET by Robert A. W. Lowndes

D-7   **PLANET OF DREAD** by Murray Leinster
       TWICE UPON A TIME by Charles L. Fontenay

D-8   **THE TERROR OUT OF SPACE** by Dwight V. Swain
       QUEST OF THE GOLDEN APE by Ivar Jorgensen and Adam Chase

D-9   **SECRET OF MARRACOTT DEEP** by Henry Slesar
       PAWN OF THE BLACK FLEET by Mark Clifton.

D-10   **BEYOND THE RINGS OF SATURN** by Robert Moore Williams
       A MAN OBSESSED by Alan E. Nourse

ARMCHAIR SCIENCE FICTION CLASSICS, $12.95 each

C-1   **THE GREEN MAN**
       by Harold M. Sherman

C-2   **A TRACE OF MEMORY**
       By Keith Laumer

C-3   **INTO PLUTONIAN DEPTHS**
       by Stanton A. Coblentz

ARMCHAIR MASTERS OF SCIENCE FICTION SERIES, $16.95 each

M-1   **MASTERS OF SCIENCE FICTION, Vol. One**
       Bryce Walton—"Dark of the Moon" and other tales

M-2   **MASTERS OF SCIENCE FICTION, Vol. Two**
       Jerome Bixby—"One Way Street" and other tales

If you've enjoyed this book, you will not want to miss these terrific titles…

ARMCHAIR SCI-FI & HORROR DOUBLE NOVELS, $12.95 each

D-11 **PERIL OF THE STARMEN** by Kris Neville
THE STRANGE INVASION by Murray Leinster

D-12 **THE STAR LORD** by Boyd Ellanby
CAPTIVES OF THE FLAME by Samuel R. Delany

D-13 **MEN OF THE MORNING STAR** by Edmund Hamilton
PLANET FOR PLUNDER by Hal Clement and Sam Merwin, Jr.

D-14 **ICE CITY OF THE GORGON** by Chester S. Geier and Richard Shaver
WHEN THE WORLD TOTTERED by Lester Del Rey

D-15 **WORLDS WITHOUT END** by Clifford D. Simak
THE LAVENDER VINE OF DEATH by Don Wilcox

D-16 **SHADOW ON THE MOON** by Joe Gibson
ARMAGEDDON EARTH by Geoff St. Reynard

D-17 **THE GIRL WHO LOVED DEATH** by Paul W. Fairman
SLAVE PLANET by Laurence M. Janifer

D-18 **SECOND CHANCE** by J. F. Bone
MISSION TO A DISTANT STAR by Frank Belknap Long

D-19 **THE SYNDIC** by C. M. Kornbluth
FLIGHT TO FOREVER by Poul Anderson

D-20 **SOMEWHERE I'LL FIND YOU** by Milton Lesser
THE TIME ARMADA by Fox B. Holden

ARMCHAIR SCIENCE FICTION CLASSICS, $12.95 each

C-4 **CORPUS EARTHLING**
by Louis Charbonneau

C-5 **THE TIME DISSOLVER**
by Jerry Sohl

C-6 **WEST OF THE SUN**
by Edgar Pangborn

ARMCHAIR SCIENCE FICTION & HORROR GEMS SERIES, $12.95 each

G-1 **SCIENCE FICTION GEMS, Vol. One**
Isaac Asimov and others

G-2 **HORROR GEMS, Vol. One**
Carl Jacobi and others

If you've enjoyed this book, you will not want to miss these terrific titles...

ARMCHAIR SCI-FI, FANTASY, & HORROR DOUBLE NOVELS, $12.95 each

D-21 **EMPIRE OF EVIL** by Robert Arnette
THE SIGN OF THE TIGER by Alan E. Nourse & J. A. Meyer

D-22 **OPERATION SQUARE PEG** by Frank Belknap Long
ENCHANTRESS OF VENUS by Leigh Brackett

D-23 **THE LIFE WATCH** by Lester Del Rey
CREATURES OF THE ABYSS by Murray Leinster

D-24 **LEGION OF LAZARUS** by Edmond Hamilton
STAR HUNTER by Andre Norton

D-25 **EMPIRE OF WOMEN** by John Fletcher
ONE OF OUR CITIES IS MISSING by Irving Cox

D-26 **THE WRONG SIDE OF PARADISE** by Raymond F. Jones
THE INVOLUNTARY IMMORTALS by Rog Phillips

D-27 **EARTH QUARTER** by Damon Knight
ENVOY TO NEW WORLDS by Keith Laumer

D-28 **SLAVES TO THE METAL HORDE** by Milton Lesser
HUNTERS OUT OF TIME by Joseph E. Kelleam

D-29 **RX JUPITER SAVE US** by Ward Moore
BEWARE THE USURPERS by Geoff St. Reynard

D-30 **SECRET OF THE SERPENT** by Don Wilcox
CRUSADE ACROSS THE VOID by Dwight V. Swain

ARMCHAIR SCIENCE FICTION CLASSICS, $12.95 each

C-7 **THE SHAVER MYSTERY, Book One**
by Richard S. Shaver

C-8 **THE SHAVER MYSTERY, Book Two**
by Richard S. Shaver

C-9 **MURDER IN SPACE** by David V. Reed
by David V. Reed

ARMCHAIR MASTERS OF SCIENCE FICTION SERIES, $16.95 each

M-3 **MASTERS OF SCIENCE FICTION, Vol. Three**
Robert Sheckley, "The Perfect Woman" and other tales

M-4 **MASTERS OF SCIENCE FICTION, Vol. Four**
Mack Reynolds, "Stowaway" and other tales

If you've enjoyed this book, you will not want to miss these terrific titles...

ARMCHAIR SCI-FI & HORROR DOUBLE NOVELS, $12.95 each

D-51   **A GOD NAMED SMITH** by Henry Slesar
           WORLDS OF THE IMPERIUM by Keith Laumer

D-52   **CRAIG'S BOOK** by Don Wilcox
           EDGE OF THE KNIFE by H. Beam Piper

D-53   **THE SHINING CITY** by Rena M. Vale
           THE RED PLANET by Russ Winterbotham

D-54   **THE MAN WHO LIVED TWICE** by Rog Phillips
           VALLEY OF THE CROEN by Lee Tarbell

D-55   **OPERATION DISASTER** by Milton Lesser
           LAND OF THE DAMNED by Berkeley Livingston

D-56   **CAPTIVE OF THE CENTAURIANESS** by Poul Anderson
           A PRINCESS OF MARS by Edgar Rice Burroughs

D-57   **THE NON-STATISTICAL MAN** by Raymond F. Jones
           MISSION FROM MARS by Rick Conroy

D-58   **INTRUDERS FROM THE STARS** by Ross Rocklynne
           FLIGHT OF THE STARLING by Chester S. Geier

D-59   **COSMIC SABOTEUR** by Frank M. Robinson
           LOOK TO THE STARS by Willard Hawkins

D-60   **THE MOON IS HELL!** by John W. Campbell, Jr.
           THE GREEN WORLD by Hal Clement

ARMCHAIR SCIENCE FICTION CLASSICS, $12.95 each

C-16   **THE SHAVER MYSTERY, Book Three**
           by Richard S. Shaver

C-17   **THE PLANET STRAPPERS**
           by Raymond Z. Gallun

C-18   **THE FOURTH "R"**
           by George O. Smith

ARMCHAIR SCIENCE FICTION & HORROR GEMS SERIES, $12.95 each

G-5   **SCIENCE FICTION GEMS, Vol. Three**
          C. M. Kornbluth and others

G-6   **HORROR GEMS, Vol. Three**
          August Derleth and others

If you've enjoyed this book, you will not want to miss these terrific titles...

ARMCHAIR SCI-FI & HORROR DOUBLE NOVELS, $12.95 each

D-61 **THE MAN WHO STOPPED AT NOTHING** by Paul W. Fairman
TEN FROM INFINITY by Ivar Jorgensen

D-62 **WORLDS WITHIN** by Rog Phillips
THE SLAVE by C.M. Kornbluth

D-63 **SECRET OF THE BLACK PLANET** by Milton Lesser
THE OUTCASTS OF SOLAR III by Emmett McDowell

D-64 **WEB OF THE WORLDS** by Harry Harrison and Katherine MacLean
RULE GOLDEN by Damon Knight

D-65 **TEN TO THE STARS** by Raymond Z. Gallun
THE CONQUERORS by David H. Keller, M. D.

D-66 **THE HORDE FROM INFINITY** by Dwight V. Swain
THE DAY THE EARTH FROZE by Gerald Hatch

D-67 **THE WAR OF THE WORLDS** by H. G. Wells
THE TIME MACHINE by H. G. Wells

D-68 **STARCOMBERS** by Edmond Hamilton
THE YEAR WHEN STARDUST FELL by Raymond F. Jones

D-69 **HOCUS-POCUS UNIVERSE** by Jack Williamson
QUEEN OF THE PANTHER WORLD by Berkeley Livingston

D-70 **BATTERING RAMS OF SPACE** by Don Wilcox
DOOMSDAY WING by George H. Smith

ARMCHAIR SCIENCE FICTION & FANTASY CLASSICS, $12.95 each

C-19 **EMPIRE OF JEGGA**
by David V. Reed

C-20 **THE TOMORROW PEOPLE**
by Judith Merril

C-21 **THE MAN FROM YESTERDAY**
by Howard Browne as by Lee Francis

C-22 **THE TIME TRADERS**
by Andre Norton

C-23 **ISLANDS OF SPACE**
by John W. Campbell

C-24 **THE GALAXY PRIMES**
by E. E. "Doc" Smith

If you've enjoyed this book, you will not want to miss these terrific titles…

ARMCHAIR SCI-FI & HORROR DOUBLE NOVELS, $12.95 each

D-71   **THE DEEP END** by Gregory Luce
        TO WATCH BY NIGHT by Robert Moore Williams

D-72   **SWORDSMAN OF LOST TERRA** by Poul Anderson
        PLANET OF GHOSTS by David V. Reed

D-73   **MOON OF BATTLE** by J. J. Allerton
        THE MUTANT WEAPON by Murray Leinster

D-74   **OLD SPACEMEN NEVER DIE!** John Jakes
        RETURN TO EARTH by Bryan Berry

D-75   **THE THING FROM UNDERNEATH** by Milton Lesser
        OPERATION INTERSTELLAR by George O. Smith

D-76   **THE BURNING WORLD** by Algis Budrys
        FOREVER IS TOO LONG by Chester S. Geier

D-77   **THE COSMIC JUNKMAN** by Rog Phillips
        THE ULTIMATE WEAPON by John W. Campbell

D-78   **THE TIES OF EARTH** by James H. Schmitz
        CUE FOR QUIET by Thomas L. Sherred

D-79   **SECRET OF THE MARTIANS** by Paul W. Fairman
        THE VARIABLE MAN by Philip K. Dick

D-80   **THE GREEN GIRL** by Jack Williamson
        THE ROBOT PERIL by Don Wilcox

ARMCHAIR SCIENCE FICTION CLASSICS, $12.95 each

C-25   **THE STAR KINGS**
        by Edmond Hamilton

C-26   **NOT IN SOLITUDE**
        by Kenneth Gantz

C-32   **PROMETHEUS II**
        by S. J. Byrne

ARMCHAIR SCIENCE FICTION & HORROR GEMS SERIES, $12.95 each

G-7   **SCIENCE FICTION GEMS, Vol. Seven**
        Jack Sharkey and others

G-8   **HORROR GEMS, Vol. Eight**
        Seabury Quinn and others